The Map

A Novel by Perry D. Jones

Synergy Books

Prologue

"The Show"

Doug E. Fresh & The Get Fresh Crew (1985)

Before I had language for grief, or God, or girls, I had the beat.

It came through a busted Panasonic radio, sitting on top of a stained microwave in a kitchen too quiet for a Saturday. I was nine. Still skinny, still hopeful. Still thinking maybe if I acted just right, my parents might stop arguing for a day. Or at least not slam so many damn doors.

Mom was in her room. Dad was somewhere else— his body maybe in the house, but his attention was always off wandering. I was in the kitchen, pouring cereal into a bowl I didn't plan to eat, when it happened.

"Six minutes... six minutes... six minutes, Doug E. Fresh you're on!"

I froze. My hand still on the cereal box. That voice—playful, wild, electric—shot through the speaker like somebody had unscrewed the lid on joy and let it loose.

Then came the beatboxing.

I'd never heard anything like it. Not on TV. Not at school. Not even from the older kids on the block who swore they were DJs because they had a boombox and a sharpie tag on their backpack.

That beat bounced like it was made of rubber and swagger. Like it didn't care what kind of morning you were having. It was going to fix it anyway.

I remember laughing out loud. Not because something was funny. But because it was *freeing*. It was like air I didn't know I'd been missing. I danced right there in the kitchen—spoon in one hand, cereal all over the floor—like the walls weren't thin and the world wasn't heavy.

That was the day I fell in love with hip hop.

It didn't come with a lecture. It didn't ask for permission. It didn't tell me to behave.

It said, *"Be loud. Be Black. Be alive."*

After that, I was never the same. I recorded the song the next time I heard it—used a blank cassette and hit record so hard I cracked the button. Played it until the tape warped. Learned every word. Tried to mimic the beatbox in the mirror until I got dizzy. When I walked to school, *that* was the rhythm in my step.

And when the fights in my house got louder, the music in my head got louder too. Not to drown it out, but to fight back.

That was the first time I understood that sound could save you.

Not religion. Not rules. *Rhythm.*

And now?

Forty years later, I still remember where I was standing. What the linoleum felt like under my feet. What my mom yelled when she saw the cereal on the floor. Even that couldn't ruin it.

Because that day, I heard something that told me:

"You matter. You belong. You got style. You got something to say."

That was the beginning of everything.

And I've been chasing that feeling ever since.

Chapter 1

"Can I Kick It?"

A Tribe Called Quest (1990)

"Can I kick it? Yes, you can"

The center opens at 8, but I show up at 6:30. That hour and a half before the world kicks in? That's mine. My ritual. My peace.

No paperwork. No teenagers talking over each other. No board members emailing me about programming outcomes or asking if we're "leveraging our digital platforms." Just me, the gym, and whatever beat I choose to start the day. Today, it's *"Can I Kick It?"*

That bassline strolls in like it's been here before. Confident. Smooth. Not in a rush to impress. I let it ride while I unlock the equipment closet and grab the broom. I've got a Bluetooth speaker clipped to my belt and Tribe bouncing off the hardwood like memory.

I sweep slow. Not because I'm trying to be precise—but because it's meditative. One hand pushing, one hand free. I move to the rhythm. The bristles whisper over the floor, picking up crumbs from yesterday's after-school scrimmage. A couple broken rubber bands, somebody's Doritos dust, a plastic bead from a girl's braids. This floor holds stories. I try to treat it like it deserves some respect.

I used to teach African American Lit at Alabama A&M. Wore sport coats and lectured about double consciousness and postmodern identity in hip hop. Had a whole unit on *Illmatic* and *The Souls of Black Folk* in the same week. My students loved it. But after a while, academia felt like a nice cage. Everything framed in rubrics. The sharp edges sanded down until nothing cut deep.

So I left. Opened this place. Named it after my father because it made grant funding easier. But really? This center's for Darius. For me. For every kid who needed somewhere to go after school that didn't treat them like a case study.

The Patterson Center for Youth & Culture. We call it "The Spot." Half of Huntsville does now. We've got a gym, a recording studio we're still building out, three multi-purpose classrooms, and an ugly-ass mural that the high school kids painted last summer. It's supposed to be Basquiat meets OutKast, but it looks like Kool-Aid spilled on a subway map. I love it anyway.

I toss the broom against the wall and grab a ball. I shoot from the elbow—clank. Rebound. Shoot again—short. My knees remind me they've got miles on them. I ignore the ache. That's part of the ritual too.

I glance at the scoreboard. Stuck at 8:46. It's been broken for years. One of the kids once asked if I kept it frozen on purpose. I said no, but maybe I should've.

That's the time I got the call about Darius.

Fifteen years and the air still changes when I say his name in my head. He was the youngest of six, all born loud and full of heat. I was an only child, raised on silences and tight-lipped tension. We met when we were four, lived next door in Charleston. First time we spoke, he tried to trade me a Now & Later for a crayon. We'd been tight ever since.

He had this gift—he could make anything feel like a joke, even pain. I watched him lose jobs, get cheated on, bury his brother—and still walk into a room like it owed him a laugh. He was the first person who ever told me I was funny. That I had rhythm. That I didn't have to act hard to be respected.

I never told him he inspired me.

And now he's gone. Heart attack at 34. Just like that.

I think about him a lot in the mornings. When it's quiet. When I'm alone enough to admit I'm still talking to him in my head.

My phone buzzes.

Text from Simone.

you good

No punctuation. No greeting. Just those two words.

She's in Tampa. Third grade teacher. I think about her in front of a classroom, patient voice, tight bun, small gold hoops like her mother used to wear. I wonder if her students know she rarely talks to her father. I wonder if she tells them about me at all.

I stare at the screen.
I type: *yeah. you?*
Backspace.
thinking about you
Backspace.
Finally: **Just starting the day. You?**

I send it. That's the best I can do today.

She responds a few minutes later:

headed to work. talk soon

I hold onto that last part—"talk soon"—like it's more than just something to say. Like it's a promise.

The gym lights flicker once, then hum fully awake. Sunlight spills in through the back windows. The music fades into the next track on the playlist— "Buggin' Out." I walk to my office to flip it back. No. I want *Can I Kick It?* again. I restart the song and turn the volume up just enough.

The front doors open at 7:15. Andre's early again. He's sixteen. Walks like he's got a record deal and a court case pending. Hoodie pulled low. He nods.

"Morning, Mr. P."

"Morning, Dre."

He drops his backpack, grabs a ball, and starts shooting like we're not even in the same room.

I watch him. His form's not bad. He's cocky, but not reckless. Reminds me of someone. A lot of someones.

The kids think I'm just here to coach or keep the peace. What they don't know is I'm here for them because *they* remind me I'm still alive. They make me feel like I haven't fully disappeared. Like there's still something to give.

Q-Tip loops back in, asking:

"Can I kick it?"

I whisper, mostly to myself:
"Yeah. You can."

I pick up the broom again and keep moving.

Chapter 2

"T.R.O.Y."

Pete Rock & CL Smooth (1992)

"I reminisce for a spell, or shall I say think back..."

There's a mural downtown, not far from the high school. I drive past it all the time but only stop when I'm feeling bold—or broken.

Today, I stop.

It's on the side of an old bodega with faded awnings and a hand-painted sign that reads *Tobacco | Snacks | Juice | Good Energy.* The mural takes up the entire wall: green outline, gold crown, headphones over an exaggerated grin. Darius. Not perfectly rendered, but unmistakable. Even in paint, he radiates that thing he always had—like he was in on the joke, and you were lucky to be near the punchline.

Below him, it says: *REMEMBER D*
That was my idea.

I lean against the hood of my car and press play on my speaker. *"T.R.O.Y."* floods the air. The horns swing in. Nostalgia hits like heat.

We were twenty when we drove to Atlanta just to eat Waffle House at 2 a.m. and see if the Dungeon Family's spirit still haunted the city. We freestyled in parking lots and laughed like we'd live forever. Darius said, *"Yo, we're gonna be legendary one day. Watch."*

He said that kind of stuff all the time. Not because he believed in fame. But because he believed in being *known*—not famous, but *felt*.

I used to think this mural was for the community. For his nieces and nephews. For the people who knew him before the suit-and-tie job, before the real world caught up. But the truth is, it's for me.

I needed him to still be on a wall somewhere. Still smiling. Still talking shit through the paint.

The beat fades. I don't replay it. Instead, I head back to The Spot.

As soon as I walk in, I feel it—the fingerprints I left all over the place that don't belong to me.

The walls in the main hallway are covered in local art, most of it crooked, taped with corners peeling. But that's how Darius would've wanted it. Raw. Real. Imperfect and loud.

In the rec room, there's a booth we built for recording demos—soundproofed with leftover carpet and foam from an old mattress. The mic hangs a little low, because Darius always said "your bars hit harder when you don't have to reach for them."

There's a bench outside the gym with a plaque: *"For D. The Coolest."*

Most folks think it's for some donor. I never corrected them. It's better that way.

I sit down in my office, lean back, and look at the bulletin board across from my desk. There's a Polaroid of Darius in a Kangol hat, holding up a peace sign with barbecue sauce on his shirt. There's a note in his handwriting that just says:
"You got a good heart, even if it's late sometimes."

He wrote that on a napkin the night after my divorce finalized. We were drunk off cheap whiskey and watching *Brown Sugar* on DVD like we were teenagers again.

I never told him he inspired me. Never said the things I should have.

And now?

Now, I build rooms in his image. Rooms where people can be loud, messy, brilliant. Rooms where I can still pretend he might walk through the door and give me hell about my busted jumper or my dusty playlist.

The door creaks. One of the new kids—Kenny—peeks in.

"Mr. P, you got any of that notebook paper?"

"Bottom drawer," I say. He nods, doesn't say thanks. I don't expect him to.

As he leaves, I catch a glimpse of the keychain hanging from his backpack. It's the same design as the mural—green outline, gold crown.

He got it from the mural unveiling. I didn't think anyone kept those.

I turn back toward the window.

My phone buzzes.

Simone. Just her name lighting up the screen is enough to shift the temperature in the room.

The message is short:

saw something today. thought of you.

That's it. No photo. No punctuation. But I know her. That's her way of sending softness without cracking her armor.

I stare at it for a minute before responding.

thanks. means more than you think.

I don't hit send right away. I just let the words sit there.

I wonder what she saw. A book? A song? A father walking his kid across the street?

The afternoon sun makes streaks across the floor. The gym is empty, but the echoes are still there. Darius laughing. Simone at five years old, dancing with her headphones on. My own voice, younger, saying things like *"I don't have time"* and *"I'm fine"* when I wasn't.

The mural is five miles away. But somehow, he's still in this room.

Chapter 3

"Ex-Girl to Next Girl"

Gang Starr (1992)

"Things change and that's the way it goes..."

The date was going fine until I started talking about Tupac.

We were sitting at this little café near campus— black-owned, artsy, with a chalkboard menu and mismatched chairs that tried real hard to look effortless. You know the kind of spot. Sunlight through dusty windows. Incense floating under the smell of oat milk and roasted beets. Nadine liked the vibe. Said it reminded her of a bookstore she used to work at in D.C.

She had on this burnt orange sweater, big hoops, and a silver ring on her index finger. Her nails were short, clean, painted with a dull gold that matched the flecks in her eyes. Everything about her felt balanced—like a person who made peace with her own contradictions.

Me? I was trying not to overthink how long it had been since I'd done this.

We started safe. Books. Travel. She told me she used to run poetry nights. I told her I used to teach Baldwin and Baraka. She raised an eyebrow.

"Black Lit? That's sexy," she said, sipping her hibiscus iced tea.

I smiled. "It was also underpaid."

She laughed. It was a good laugh—genuine, like it didn't need an audience.

Then came music.

"So who's your number one?" she asked, tapping the bottom of her glass.

I didn't even blink. "Tribe."

She cocked her head. "Over Pac?"

"Pac gave me truth. Tribe gave me life."

Her lips curled slightly, amused. "You don't think truth *is* life?"

"I think sometimes you need joy before you can even process truth."

We sat with that.

She nodded slowly. "Fair."

Then she said, "I dated a guy once who had a Nas lyric for everything. Whole relationship felt like a mixtape. I'd be mad and he'd just quote *'No Idea's Original.'*"

I grinned. "Respectfully, that's hilarious."

She laughed too, but it lingered at the edge of something unsaid.

Somewhere between the avocado toast and the check, the shift happened.

Not dramatic. Just… air leaving the room.

She asked, "What do you want now?"

I blinked.

"I mean in general. From life. From someone else. From yourself."

"I'm still figuring that out," I said, honest.

She gave me this look—not mean, not unkind. Just… tired. Not from me. From the game. From the way middle-aged dating is one long audition for people who forgot how to clap.

"I hope you do," she said. Then smiled. Then changed the subject.

We walked out together. Hugged. Said the polite version of "maybe again."

But we both knew.

No callback.

And honestly? I wasn't even disappointed. Just... hollow. Like I didn't swing and miss—I never even picked up the bat.

That night, I sat on the edge of my bed and scrolled through old photos on my phone. I don't have many left. Lost most of them when I dropped my phone in a puddle two years ago. I remember trying to save it like it was a drowning child.

But I kept a few. One of Simone stands out.

She's maybe ten. Wearing a sequined purple shirt, holding a kid's karaoke mic like she's about to headline a festival. Big headphones on. Her smile is crooked—her left front tooth still growing in. The kind of moment you think you'll always remember, until you forget what day it happened.

I remember it, though.
I remember Rhonda standing behind her, just barely

in frame, holding the camera. Her laugh in the background. Simone bouncing on her heels like a boxer before a fight.

"Daddy, can I do my song now?" she asked.

"Only if it's clean," I said.

Rhonda rolled her eyes. "Let her talk, Malik."

Simone rapped for two minutes straight. Rhymed "teacher" with "preacher," and said something about flying to New York and being on BET.

After she finished, she looked at me with this wide, expectant grin. That kid kind of pride—so big it fills the room and dares you not to clap.

And I ruined it.

"It was good," I said. "But next time try writing something with a message."

I thought I was teaching.

But I was doing what I always did: filtering everything through critique. Measuring joy with a ruler.

She never performed again.

I pull up Simone's name in my messages. Scroll through our last few texts. None of them longer than a sentence or two. No emojis. No calls. Just maintenance.

You good?
Headed to work.
Okay. Be safe.

I want to text her something real. Something like, *I still see that little girl in the purple shirt every time I hear a beat.*

Instead, I close the app.

Coward move.

But familiar.

The next morning at the center, I'm half awake. Sorting basketballs, dealing with a crick in my neck from sleeping wrong. The gym smells like sweat and cheap plastic. The first few kids trickle in.

Andre strolls up. Hoodie. Slides. No socks. Same as always.

"You go on that date?" he asks, smirking like he already knows.

I pause. "Who told you?"

"My aunt told my mom who told my cousin who told me."

"And?"

"You blew it, didn't you?"

I snort. "You always this encouraging?"

"I'm just saying, Mr. P—maybe you need a new playlist."

He grins and jogs off. I shake my head.

Later, when the noise dies down and I'm sweeping the court, I play *Gang Starr* on my speaker. "Ex-Girl to Next Girl." That beat slaps a little too hard for how soft I'm feeling. I let it ride.

I'm not trying to be a player. Never was.

But I've played myself enough to know the difference.

And now?

I don't want the next girl.

I want to be the next version of me.

Chapter 4

"Electric Relaxation"

A Tribe Called Quest (1993)

"I like 'em brown, yellow, Puerto Rican or Haitian..."

She walks into The Spot like she already knows where everything is.

Not in a loud or attention-hungry way—more like the air parts for her. Like the building recognizes her spirit.

She's here for a potential partnership—a wellness program through one of the local nonprofits. Weekly group sessions for teens dealing with loss, pressure, identity. The quiet kind of trauma that sits in the chest like extra weight. The kind of pain no one wants to name but everyone carries.

She asked for a meeting before committing. Said she needed to feel the *energy* of the place.

I didn't roll my eyes, but I almost did.
I've heard that line before—from over-eager grad

students with crystals in their pockets and no idea what this community really needs.

But something about the way she said it made me pause.

So I said yes.

I'm in the conference room when she walks in— five minutes early.

She's wearing a navy blue t-shirt with the words *"still healing. still here."* in lowercase white script. Simple. Direct. Like a thesis statement. Her jeans are cuffed, sneakers plain, and she's got long, black braids pulled back into a low ponytail.

No earrings. No fake smile.

When she offers her hand, I take it. Her grip is confident. Her palm warm.

"Mr. Patterson?" she asks.

"Malik," I say.

Her eyes hold mine just a second longer than necessary. Not testing me. Just present.

She opens a small notebook—lined paper, black ink. No tablet. No buzzwords.

She talks with ease. Clear, but not rehearsed. She explains the workshop: a blend of mindfulness, movement, journaling, and music. Not therapy, exactly. More like emotional CPR. A way to give these kids *language* for the chaos they've been handed.

"Most of them don't need fixing," she says. "They need translation. They've got all these feelings—anger, confusion, joy—but no dictionary."

I nod, slower than usual. "We try to hold space here. Not just keep kids busy."

She smiles. "That's obvious. You can feel it. Someone cared about this place."

The comment hangs in the room. Not heavy. But not light either.

Because she's right.

Everything here is intentional—even if I never say it out loud.

The acoustic panels lining the multipurpose room? I chose them because I thought, *Darius would've picked these. Bright, absorbent. Soft on the outside, strong underneath.*
He's been gone fifteen years, but I still hear his

laugh when I walk through this place. Still wonder what he'd roast me about if he could see the ugly-ass mural the kids painted last summer.

We talk logistics. Dates, space needs, waivers. Then she asks if she can walk through the gym.

I take her down the hallway, past the art wall— layers of student work overlapping like time stamps. As we pass, I notice her eyes scanning the work. Not just looking—*reading*. Like she's cataloging what's here and what's missing.

When we step into the gym, the echo hits.

It's empty. Just the buzz of the overhead lights and the sound of Tribe playing low over the speakers.

She stops and tilts her head. Smiles.

"Midnight Marauders," she says.

I raise an eyebrow. "You know that on the first note?"

"Of course. I don't trust people who say they love hip hop but can't place the roots."

I chuckle. "That's fair."

She walks toward center court, slow, then stops and closes her eyes. Breathes. Her hands at her sides, relaxed. She's not performing—she's just *feeling*.

"You always play music in here?" she asks without opening her eyes.

"When I'm alone," I say.

She opens her eyes. "This place has good energy."

The way she says it—it's not fluff. Not New Age nonsense. It's felt. Observed. Real.

I almost want to tell her the truth—that this gym is built out of ghosts and grief and grit. That I measure time here in mistakes and small miracles. That I still see my daughter's sneakers squeaking on this floor, even though she hasn't been back in years.

But I don't say any of that. I just nod.

We keep walking. She points to a quote painted above the door in uneven brush strokes.

"Be louder than your silence."

"You come up with that?" she asks.

"No," I say. "One of the kids did. I just gave him the wall."

She lets that linger, then says, "That's good leadership."

I look at her. "It's just presence."

She turns to face me. "That's the part most people skip."

Twenty minutes pass. Then thirty. We talk about her group facilitation style, how she doesn't push kids to share before they're ready. About how her last workshop led to one of her students writing their first poem about their father—someone they'd only ever called "him."

I ask what got her into this work.

She shrugs. "My own need for it, probably."

That's all she says.

I don't press.

As she's leaving, she turns to me in the doorway.

"You ever host any adult workshops?" she asks.

"Not yet."

"Maybe you should. This place feels like it could hold grown folks too."

I smile. "I'll think about it."

She nods and walks out. Braids swinging. No extra words.

When she's gone, I sit on the bench by the door and let the album play through.

Electric Relaxation rolls in like a wave. I know every word, every ad-lib. But today, I don't sing along.

I just *feel it.*

There's a stillness I haven't let myself enjoy in years.

Not attraction. Not fantasy.
Just ease.
And that's harder to come by than anything else.

I don't know her name yet.
But I know the rhythm she walked in with.

And I know that if I'm ever going to learn how to be *seen*, it's going to start here—

in the quiet between verses.

Chapter 5

"Children's Story"

Slick Rick (1988)

"He was only seventeen, in a madman's dream..."

The phone call came at 7:42 a.m.

I was standing in the staff kitchen, staring down the slowest damn coffee maker in Alabama, when Celeste poked her head in.

"You might wanna talk to Andre," she said.

I didn't flinch. Just took a sip of hot water pretending to be coffee.

"What happened?"

"He punched a kid. Not play-punched. Real-punched."

By the time I got to the main hallway, Andre was sitting on the bench near the lockers, hoodie up, headphones around his neck, one sneaker off like he left in a hurry. He looked less mad than tired.

The other kid had already been picked up. According to Celeste, it wasn't as bad as it sounded. "Mostly chest shots. No blood."

I sat down next to him—not close, but not far enough to feel like a scolding.

"You good?" I asked.

Shrug.

"You wanna tell me what happened?"

"Not really."

Silence. Long enough for the overhead lights to buzz into it.

Then, just under his breath: "He said something about my mom."

I nodded. "What'd he say?"

Andre's jaw tightened. "Called her a crackhead. Said that's why I'm always broke and angry."

The words pulled something out of me.

Something buried.

I saw myself at fifteen—standing in the cafeteria line at Stall High School in Charleston. Kid in front of me mimicked my mom's voice. Thick Gullah accent, slow and warm, like syrup on the tongue.

He said, *"Yuh mudduh talk like she chew'n watah."*

Everyone laughed.

I didn't.

I dropped my tray and swung. Hit him square in the chest. He stumbled, fell, called me a freak. I tried to hit him again, but Coach Simmons pulled me back before I did something permanent.

My mom didn't speak to me the whole ride home. Just stared out the window, knuckles tight on the wheel.

When we got to the house, she said, *"Don't let nobody pull yuh down in duh mud wit dem."*

I wanted her to be mad at him. I wanted her to say I was right.

Instead, she was just disappointed.

But my dad?

Gerald didn't even look up from his paper when she told him. Just said, "Should've made sure the kid stayed down." Then went back to reading.

That's how he always was—emotion muted, love expressed through old-school logic and a steady paycheck. I never heard him say "I'm proud of you." Not once.

Back in the present, I looked at Andre.

"Is it true?" he asked. "What he said about my mom?"

"She works nights at the hospital," I said. "Sends you with lunch and a book every time you leave this building."

He didn't say anything. Just blinked slow.

"She's trying," I added.

He stared at the floor. His leg was bouncing—agitated, like he wanted to run somewhere but didn't know where.

I opened the door to my office and motioned for him to follow.

Once inside, I flipped on my speaker and queued up *"Children's Story."*

The beat spilled out—light, bouncing, deceptive in its playfulness.

Andre wrinkled his nose. "You always play old music when you're mad?"

I smiled. "Only when I'm trying to remind myself what I didn't learn soon enough."

I handed him a cold bottle of water and sat across from him.

"Tenth grade," I said. "I almost got expelled for hitting a kid who mocked my mom's voice. Gullah accent. Said she sounded like a cartoon character."

"Damn," he muttered.

"I hit him hard. Knocked the wind out of him."

"Did you regret it?"

"Later. When the noise died down."

"What happened?"

"My mom wouldn't look at me for two days. My dad said I should've hit harder. I didn't know who to listen to."

He was quiet. Then said: "What do you think now?"

I let the question sit there.

"I think violence feels like power when you don't know how to use your voice," I said.

He nodded like he understood that. Too well.

I pulled a notebook from my drawer—plain black cover, a little worn on the edges—and slid it across the desk.

"You write?"

"A little," he mumbled.

"Write this down. Not for school. For you."

"What if I don't want to?"

"That's cool," I said. "Just don't come crying when I start ghostwriting your life."

That got a small grin. Barely there. But it counted.

He grabbed the notebook, tucked it under his hoodie, and walked out without another word.

After he left, I sat in the quiet.

The song played out, and I let it loop again.

I thought about the kid I used to be.
The mother I didn't defend with words.

The father I couldn't reach with silence.
The daughter who got the unfinished version of me.

Simone was in eighth grade when she told me she wanted to be a writer.

I bought her a grammar workbook.

She never brought it up again.

I looked around the room—at the photos on the wall, the Post-Its from kids past and present, the chair where Andre sat.

There's a part of me I only meet in this room.

The part that's still fifteen, fists clenched, waiting to be told who he's supposed to be.

I turned the music up.

Let Rick finish the story.

Then started it over again.

Because this time, I wanted to *listen*.

Chapter 6

"Respiration"

Black Star (1998)

"Breathe in. Breathe out. Breathe in…"

My father owns four cars.

He's seventy-three, retired, and allergic to socializing, but still rotates them like he's running a shop with imaginary customers.

"Gotta keep the blood moving," he always says.

I stopped arguing about it years ago.

His garage is already open when I pull up. Sun hasn't fully committed yet—just that early-morning brightness that makes the asphalt look alive. I park at the curb, like always. Never in the driveway. That's *his* space, and I know better.

The lineup's unchanged:

- The **El Camino** on jack stands, one wheel off
- The **Camry** crooked on the lawn
- The **Cadillac** untouched, except for the thick layer of yellow pollen
- The **Mustang** under a tarp, his "maybe this year" project for the last six years

My **2020 Honda Accord Sport** idles quietly at the curb. Not flashy. Not fast. But it's clean, black, and rides smooth.

I've only ever driven Hondas. Tribute.

Darius's whole family swore by them. His mom, his sisters, even his uncle who claimed he was "too smooth for a Civic" drove one eventually. Darius used to say, *"A Honda gets you where you're going. That's enough."*

After he passed, I never considered anything else.

Gerald once called it "basic." Said, *"You could've at least got a truck."*

I didn't argue. Some things you don't explain. You just drive.

"Morning," I say, stepping into the garage.

He's halfway under the hood of the El Camino. Doesn't look up. "You're early."

"You called me."

He grunts. "Didn't expect you to come the same day."

That's how he does affection—accusatory.

We don't talk for the first ten minutes. I hand him tools he doesn't ask for, and he critiques them anyway. He doesn't need help—he just doesn't want to be alone. But he'll never admit that.

The **garage has its own rhythm**:

- The radio is always tuned to AM talk, volume low.
- There's a fan in the corner that clicks every third rotation.
- Tools are organized like a museum display—each socket in its assigned velvet bed.
- An oil-stained towel hangs from a hook like a flag.

Every time I come, I find a new project in mid-surgery.

And every time I leave, something else has been fixed that wasn't broken.

"You're rotating your tires?" he asks, not looking up.

"You ask me that every visit."

"You always say no."

"I do rotate them," I lie.

"Not enough."

I glance at the El Camino. "You ever think about selling a couple of these?"

He wipes sweat from his brow. "You ever think about minding your business?"

Fair.

Inside, the house hasn't changed since 1992. Maybe earlier.

Same chipped Formica table. Same fridge magnets. Same recliner with the left arm fraying from years of fingernails and football games. Same clock that ticks loud enough to remind you life is passing but quiet enough not to feel threatening.

He pours us both a cup of coffee. No cream. No sugar. Slides one across the table.

That's his love language. *Black coffee in silence.*

"You still running that center?" he asks, settling into the recliner.

"Yeah. Growing, actually."

"Growing how?"

"More kids. More programs. Got someone coming in to run a mental health workshop."

He snorts. "That new age stuff."

"It's real, Dad."

He doesn't argue. Just sips his coffee and stares out the window like it might offer a rebuttal.

We sit for a while, the house humming with silence and decades of stubbornness.

I break it first.

"Remember when I got suspended in high school? For fighting?"

He doesn't move. "You hit some kid over something he said about your mother."

"Yeah. Said she sounded like she had marbles in her mouth."

His jaw tightens. "She was proud of that voice."

"I know."

"She tried to sand it down once. For a job interview. I told her not to."

I blink. That's a new story. One he's never told me.

"She kept her accent for you," he adds. "Didn't want you thinking it was something to hide."

I don't know what to say to that.

So I sip my coffee and let it land.

He shifts in his chair. "Your mom would've liked what you're doing now. At the center."

I look at him. "You don't?"

He doesn't answer. Just sips.
Then: "I don't get it. But I don't have to."

It's the closest thing to *I'm proud of you* I've ever gotten from him.

And somehow, it's enough.

We finish the coffee. I get up to leave.

He follows me outside and stops at my car.

"You check the fluids?"

"I do regular maintenance, Dad."

"That a yes?"

"That's a 'you're gonna check them anyway.'"

He smirks. Pops the hood. Already halfway into a lecture about air filters.

I watch him while he works.

Bent over the engine. Grease on his shirt. Muscle memory in his hands.

He's never fixed the things between us with words. But he's fixed *everything else.*

Maybe that's how he apologizes.

Maybe that's how he loves.

The drive back is quiet.

I don't play music.

I just roll the window down and let the wind take
some of the weight.

I breathe in.
Breathe out.

And let the silence mean something different this
time.

Chapter 7

"The Light"

Common (2000)

"There are times when you need someone / I will be by your side…"

The rec room isn't supposed to be this loud before 9 a.m.

Usually, it's a quiet start—fluorescent lights buzzing, folded chairs stacked against the wall, and whatever lo-fi jazz the morning custodian's phone can handle playing quietly in the background.

But today?

Today it's **Juvenile**.

And not the radio stuff either.

Track sixteen. "400 Degreez."
The title track. The one with *heat* in the pocket. The one with bass so thick it rattles the windows in your teeth.

I follow the sound like it owes me something. I'm already forming the sentence—*Could you turn it down a bit?*—when I round the corner and stop cold.

She's here. Setting up. Moving slow but deliberate, like every yoga mat has a story. Like the space itself deserves care.

She's not singing along. Not dancing.

She's just *in it*.

Focused. Calm. And absolutely letting this beat ride.

I pause in the doorway, arms folded.

She doesn't look up.

"You don't like bounce music?" she says, without missing a beat.

"I didn't say anything."

"You didn't have to."

Now she looks at me. A sideways glance, half-grin tugging at the edge of her mouth. Not smug. Just **knowing**.

Like she read the whole paragraph forming in my head and decided to skip to the punchline.

I nod toward the speaker.

"'400 Degreez,' huh?"

She shrugs. "Sometimes that's the only temperature that makes sense."

Then back to the mats. Unfold. Adjust. Check spacing. Each move part of a system I don't fully understand—but respect.

She's got braids pulled back into a low ponytail. A slate-gray tee with *soft doesn't mean weak* written across the front in lowercase. Clean sneakers. No earrings. No apology in her energy.

There's a table behind her stacked with supplies:
– Laminated handouts
– Floor plans
– Color-coded Sharpies
– Journals
– A bowl of polished river stones
– A gold bell the size of a plum

Everything feels intentional. Like someone built a classroom, a studio, and a sanctuary and set them to the same beat.

I nod toward the handouts.
"Urban planner stuff?"

"Technically," she says. "These days I do less building, more listening."

She finally stands upright, wipes her hands on her jeans.

"Where'd you study?" I ask.

"Howard."

I raise an eyebrow. "Howard, Howard?"

She smirks. "You say that like there's more than one."

I laugh. "Fair. So... Mobile to D.C., then back to Alabama?"

"Sometimes where you start matters more than where you land," she says, adjusting a corner of a mat. "And sometimes you come back on purpose."

That line sticks with me.
It's not a flex.
It's just true.

And I realize I don't know why she's here—
Huntsville. The way she moves, the way she
listens—she could be anywhere. But she's here.
And now I want to know what brought her back.

But I don't ask.

Yet.

A new track starts—*"Ha."* That unmistakable beat.
Southern. Sticky. Timeless.

I shake my head. "Is this… therapeutic?"

She doesn't miss a beat. "Depends on who's
listening."

The first student walks in. Then another. She greets
each one by name, asks how they slept, asks what
their body feels like today.

And they respond.

Not like they're performing. Like they've already decided this room is safe. And she didn't demand it—she designed it.

I sit on the edge of a folding chair and watch.

I should leave. I've got emails. A city council check-in. Two parents who want to reschedule meetings they never confirmed.

But I stay.

Because watching her work is like listening to a beat you forgot you loved.

One of the students, a girl named Trinity, about thirteen, raises her hand mid-session.

"Miss, how come you got stones and not candles?"

She smiles. "Candles are fire. Stones are earth. Sometimes you don't need to burn through something—you need to hold onto it."

The girl nods like she got an answer to a question she didn't even know she'd asked.

Back in my office, I sit down and stare at my phone for a minute.

Tribe is queued up.
Low End Theory, my usual go-to.

But today, I scroll.

Find *400 Degreez*. Track sixteen.

I let it play.

Let it knock.

And for once, I don't overthink what it means.

Interlude

"Voicemails and Volume"

It's just past 9 p.m. when I call Simone.

I don't plan to. I've been sitting on the edge of my bed for twenty minutes, flipping through playlists and making excuses. But something about the workshop this morning—the way those kids opened up when someone gave them language—it stirred something in me I haven't named yet.

So I hit dial.

She picks up on the fourth ring.

"Hey," she says. Not surprised. Not cold either. Just Simone. Even.

"Hey. You busy?"

"Just grading. What's up?"

"I was just checking in."

"Mm-hmm."

She always does that.
The **"mm-hmm"** that says *I'm listening*, but also *let's not pretend this isn't rare.*

"You good?" I ask.

"I'm alright. Kids were wild today. One of them tried to convince me the Underground Railroad was a real train."

"Technically…"

"Don't even."

We both laugh.

There's a pause. Not tense. Just waiting.

"You seeing anyone?" I ask, casual but careful. The kind of question you rehearse before you ask it.

There's a beat.

"Wow," she says. "Look at you."

"Look at me what?"

"Dipping your toe into parental intimacy. Love that for you."

I smile. "You gonna answer the question or give me a PowerPoint?"

She exhales. "I'm seeing someone. Kind of."

I nod, even though she can't see it.

"Cool. Just making sure *they* know you're smarter than them."

There's a pause. She catches it.

"They do," she says, voice soft but certain.

I don't push.
And she doesn't elaborate.
But the door opens. Quietly. Just a crack.

And I know better than to slam it with a follow-up.

"You still got that purple notebook?" I ask, shifting the weight.

She's quiet for a second.

"The one from when I was little?"

"Yeah. You used to write raps in it."

"I might still have it. Somewhere."

"Cool."

"Why?"

"No reason."

Another pause. This one warmer.

"I liked that one line you wrote," I say. "The BET line."

She lets out a laugh. "That was not even a bar, Dad. That was baby rhymebook energy."

"It was *your* voice," I say. "I just didn't know how to hear it back then."

Another beat. She doesn't say anything.

Then: "Thanks."

Just that.

We stay on the line a little longer. No one rushing to hang up.

"Alright," I say eventually. "I'll let you get back to it."

"Talk soon?"

"Yeah. Soon."

I hang up.

Sit in the quiet.

Think about how much I don't know.

And how much I'm finally ready to learn.

Chapter 8

"C.R.E.A.M."

Wu-Tang Clan (1993)

"Cash rules everything around me…"

The meeting's at 11 a.m., but the grant officer shows up at 10:42, all teeth and urgency.

His name's **Austin**, but he pronounces it like *Ahh-stin*, like he studied abroad in Switzerland and thinks that gives him extra vowels.

Slim gray suit. No tie. White loafers. The kind of guy who says "community is everything" and then talks for 45 minutes without asking anyone in the room what they need.

He smiles like he's done me a favor just by showing up.

"Malik," he says, gripping my hand like I'm a podium he's trying to steady himself on. "Been hearing amazing things about The Spot. Truly inspired by what y'all are doing here."

He doesn't mean it.
Not fully.
It's that grant-speak. High-gloss empathy.

We walk through the building. He asks a lot of questions—stats, metrics, conversion rates—but doesn't really absorb the answers.

"You ever think about scaling this?"
"You tracking emotional growth by semester?"
"You run digital assessments or just anecdotal outcomes?"

When I don't answer fast enough, he fills in his own blanks.

In the gym, he points at the mural the high schoolers painted last summer. Vibrant. Messy. Beautiful.

"Love that. Very street. We're all about that aesthetic—authentic grit."

I bite my tongue. Don't tell him this mural was built from loss. From a kid we buried. From a girl who stopped speaking after her cousin got locked up. From Darius.

Not *grit*.
Grief.

We sit down in my office and that's when he lays it out.

Six-figure grant. Multi-year. Infrastructure, digital resources, expansion. The works.

The catch?

It comes through a corporate partnership with a tech startup that's built to "enhance learning environments" using AI-driven content and behavioral data collection.

"We're not trying to change what you do," Austin says. "We're trying to *amplify* it. Just give you better tools to track growth. Streamline outcomes."

The pitch has polish. I've heard it before. At other centers. Other rooms.

Those "tools" come with branded software. Pre-written lesson plans. Mandatory surveys. Data dashboards that reduce our kids to performance reports and "mood indicators."

"What kind of data are you collecting?" I ask.

He smiles like he's proud of the answer.

"Attendance patterns. Sentiment tracking. Keyword analysis. Early-intervention alerts. Nothing invasive—just predictive."

"Will the kids know they're being tracked?"

He waves it off. "Of course. Transparency is key. But kids today, they don't even notice. They're on phones all day anyway."

That's the line that gets me.

The **casual erasure** baked into that sentence. The way he assumes that surveillance and access are the same thing.

He sees them as data points.
I see them as people trying to breathe.

After he leaves, I sit in the gym alone. Let the silence settle like dust.

Then I cue up *C.R.E.A.M.*

The beat kicks in like an old friend with a bitter smile.

"Cash rules everything around me…"

And I let it ride.

I've seen what this kind of deal does to places like this.
Places that start with soul, but end up sanitized.
Centers that trade storytelling circles for behavior reports.
Art programs that get "rebranded" into "cultural competency modules."
Board members who say *"We need to modernize"* while slowly erasing the very thing that made the space sacred.

Last year, a sister program across town closed. Quietly. Got bought out by a "community impact accelerator." Their poetry night became "youth narrative alignment workshops." The snack room became a vending machine corridor.

The kids stopped coming.
The staff started quitting.
The spirit died.

I call an emergency board meeting.

Some of them already know the numbers.
Some of them are tired.

Some of them think we can take the money and
resist the terms.

I can feel the energy in the room splintering.

"There's always compromise," one member says.
"We can't serve kids with empty pockets."

"But what are we giving up in the process?" I ask.

No one answers.

I think about Simone.
About how I used to talk over her joy trying to
make it *productive*.
How I used to think love meant fixing things
instead of *holding space for them* to grow.

Now I've got a room full of people asking if we can
package love into metrics.

And I'm the one who has to say no.

That night, I go back to the office.
Flip through the packet Austin left.

There's a page titled **"Scalable Human Outcomes."**
There's a flow chart of emotions.
A formula for "resilience readiness."
A color-coded table for tracking empathy.

I close the folder.
Put it in the trash.
Turn the lights off.

In the dark, I walk to the free throw line.

Shoot with no ball.

Form. Release. Follow through.

Over and over.

Because some things are worth repeating until they're automatic.

Chapter 9

"Umi Says"

Mos Def (1999)

"I want Black people to be free / to be free, to be free…"

I haven't been back to Charleston in four years.

Every time I almost go, something stops me.
A deadline. A flat tire. A reason that's really just an excuse wrapped in routine.

Because I know what that city does to me.

How the streets echo too loud.
How the air gets thick with memory.
How even the church pews feel like old skin I can't slip back into.

But tonight?

Tonight, Charleston comes to me.

Not in a dream.

In a sound.
In a voice.
In a pull I can't ignore.

It's almost 10 p.m. I'm on the couch. Lights off. The hum of the streetlight outside barely touches the living room.

I scroll to *"Umi Says."*

Let it play.

Let it wash over me.

The guitar sneaks in first. Then that heartbeat of a bassline. Then Mos's voice—clear, prayerful, like he's talking to God and us at the same time.

"I want Black people to be free..."

I close my eyes.

And suddenly—

I'm back there.

Charleston.
St. James AME.
Graveyard tucked behind the church like it's hiding
from the highway noise.
The smell of pine sap and summer rain in the dirt.
The gravestone is simple. Gray. No flourishes.

Just her name: **Mariama Jean Patterson.**
The year she came in. The year she left.

And the line I chose:
"She made peace feel possible."

I remember asking her what her name meant.

She said, *"Mariama come from across duh watah.
It mean gift, or grace. People name dey chilrun fo'
what dey hope dem to be."*

Then she smiled that tired smile of hers—the one
that lived between sorrow and certainty—and said,
*"My mama hoped I'd bring calm into things. But
sometimes I brought fire first."*

That name always held weight.
Sounded like scripture when she said it.
Still does.

I kneel beside the grave.

Run my hand across the stone. It's cold, even in the heat.

"Hey, Ma."

The wind doesn't answer. But something moves in the trees.

I don't talk to her often—not like this.

I pray. I remember.

But this? This kind of talking? It takes more out of me than I like to admit.

I take a deep breath, like I need permission.

And then I say it.

"I'm tired."

I tell her about the center.

About the offer I turned down—the tech money that came with strings and silence.

I tell her about the board, half of them ready to vote me out if I don't pivot.

I tell her about the kids—how some days I see
versions of myself in them that I'm not proud of.

I tell her about Simone.

That she's teaching in Tampa.
That she's got someone in her life.
That I think I'm finally starting to be the kind of
father she might forgive one day.

I tell her about this woman I haven't named yet.
That she moves like a blueprint.
Talks like she knows where the roots are buried.
And makes me feel like softness isn't a weakness,
but a doorway.

I pause.

The silence feels full.

Like a quilt being pulled over me.

I remember her voice.
That **Gullah rhythm** that made everything sound
like a blessing and a warning at the same time.

When I was little, I used to lay in bed listening to
her talk on the phone in the next room—low,

steady, words I didn't always understand, but tone I could feel in my chest.

I remember when a teacher once told me I should *"translate my mother's accent"* during parent night.

I didn't fight back.

I just went quiet.

When I told her what the teacher said, she looked at me and said,
"Ain't nothin' wrong wit duh way I speak. Dey just ain't used to hearing home."

She used to hum when she cooked. Never full songs. Just pieces. A line here. A chord there.

Spirituals. Old soul. Sometimes jazz.

Once—I'll never forget this—she was doing dishes and humming *"Keep Ya Head Up."*

I asked her why she was singing Tupac.

She didn't even blink.

Said, *"He was hurting. Same way your daddy was. Same way you will one day."*

Then she dried her hands and kissed my forehead.

I don't cry.

But my breath stutters.

I tell her I'm trying.

That I'm building something.

That I hope she'd be proud.

That I still don't have all the words for the ache I carry.

But I'm learning.

I sit in that space for a long time.

Not quite prayer. Not quite memory.

Just me, her, and the music playing soft from the speaker.

"I want my people to be free, to be free, to be free..."

Eventually, the track ends.

But the air still feels holy.

I open my eyes.

Back in Huntsville.
Back in my living room.
The weight in my chest... not gone, but *shifted*.

Lighter.

Centered.

Like maybe her peace has finally found its way
through the walls I built.

I sit in the quiet a while longer.

Not to escape it.

To **honor it**.

Because not all healing comes in storms.

Sometimes it just shows up as a song you forgot
you needed—

until you finally let it play all the way through.

Chapter 10

"Memory Lane"

Nas (1994)

"I rap for listeners, blunt heads, fly ladies and prisoners..."

I wasn't looking for anything when I found it.

Just cleaning. Avoiding everything else by pretending I'm doing something useful. The kind of chore you do when you're avoiding people, meetings, decisions—life.

Middle desk drawer. Bottom stack. Under a few old church programs and a pack of AA batteries I forgot I bought.

A CD-R.
Silver. Sharpie-scribbled.
"God's Son / Stillmatic mix – D."

My stomach drops a little.

It's been at least a decade since I saw this disc. But the handwriting is unmistakable—slanted and too neat to belong to someone who lived as wild as Darius did.

He used to make these like some people write letters.

Never just playlists. Always mixes with a purpose. A narrative. A thesis.

This one was from the year he got his second teaching job. He said he was going through something and needed Nas to walk him through it.

I never asked what the "something" was.
I figured if he needed to say it out loud, he would've put it in a bar.

I plug in the old USB CD drive I keep for nostalgia and half-finished projects. The drive hums like it's waking from surgery.

Track one: *"Memory Lane (Sittin' in da Park)."*

Of course.

The beat drops—warm, nostalgic, crackling like a dusty needle on vinyl.

"I rap for listeners, blunt heads, fly ladies and prisoners..."

And suddenly—

Darius is here.

Not as a ghost.

As a **presence**.

We're seventeen again.

Sittin' in his room, sun sliding through busted blinds, fan in the window humming loud like it's arguing with the heat.

He's on the floor with a spiral notebook and a pen with no cap.
I'm posted on the edge of the bed, shoes off, elbows on my knees.
The Source magazine open between us.

We're not just listening—we're **studying**.

We treat Nas like scripture.

"I rap for listeners..."

He pauses the track. Rewinds.

"That line covers *everyone*," he says. "But who's left out?"

We'd do that for hours—take one verse and stretch it into philosophy.

Darius didn't just love Nas.

He believed in him.

Said, *"If Pac was fire and Big was weight, then Nas is light. You see through it and by it."*

I didn't argue.
Not because I agreed.
But because I liked watching him work it out.

Track two starts: *"Nas Is Like."*

That Primo drop punches through like a drumline on its best day.

"Freedom or jail, clips inserted..."

Darius would quote that line like a gospel intro.

"This ain't a song," he once told me. "It's a preamble. He's laying down truth before he even finishes the first bar."

We used to walk around Alabama A&M like we were carrying something holy in our backpacks.

Not just books.
Notebooks.

Ours. His. Nas's.
Any line worth remembering got underlined, scribbled, dissected.

"Nas is like Iron Mike, messiah type / Before the Christ, after the death…"

He stopped the track there once.

Said, "That's the bar."

"What about it?"

"That's how I wanna write," he said. "Like I got a past *and* a prophecy in every line."

That's who Darius was.

Not just a dreamer. Not just a lyric-lover.

He wanted to live like the music meant something.
Like it could explain the world if you just listened
hard enough.

When he died, I couldn't listen to Nas for six
months.

Couldn't play *It Was Written.*
Couldn't hear *"The World Is Yours"* without
feeling like mine wasn't.

Not because the music hurt.
But because it remembered.

The CD keeps playing.

Track three is *"No Idea's Original."*
I smile at that. That was one of our biggest debates.

I used to say Nas was recycling himself.

Darius would say, *"Nah. He's revisiting. There's a
difference."*

That's what I'm doing now.

Revisiting.

Simone had sent the CD earlier in the week. Said she found a shoebox in storage from her mom's garage.

"It had this old disc with Uncle Darius' name on it. I thought you should have it."

She was right.

It always belonged here.

I pause the track and open an old drawer. Pull out one of Darius' notebooks.

First page: his name. His signature slanted left like it was leaning into the wind.

Second page:

"One day, we gone break down every line in 'One Mic.' Word for word."

I close it gently.
Place it next to the CD.

Like I'm arranging an altar.

I sit there, letting the silence settle.
Letting the ghost of our arguments and laughter curl around me like smoke.

I don't say anything out loud.

But I know if Darius were here, he'd play *"Memory Lane"* again.

Then pause it.

Then ask, "You catch that?"

And I'd say, "Not yet."

And he'd say, "Then play it again."

Interlude

"The Truth"

Pharoahe Monch (1999)

"Truth is, I always wanted to be that fly..."

She doesn't knock.

She just steps into the doorway of my office, a tea in one hand, binder in the other, and that look on her face like she already knows I'm spinning out before I say anything.

"You good?" she asks.

It's not casual.

It's surgical.

I look up. Nod.

She sets the tea down on my desk. Chamomile. Always chamomile. She swears it's for anxiety, even though I've never seen her anything but composed.

"Something on your mind," she says, more of a statement than a question.

I look at the clock.
It's late.
Center's quiet.
Doors locked.
No kids.
No board.
Just her and me.

I say, "You ever lose somebody and feel like the world kept all their sounds, but none of their weight?"

She pauses.

Then: "Every day for about two years straight."

She sits in the chair across from me. Doesn't touch the tea. Doesn't cross her arms.

Just sits.

Present.

I take a breath.

Tell her about the CD.

About Darius.

About how we used to sit in hot dorm rooms and break down Nas like we were prepping for trial.

She smiles. Not out of nostalgia. Out of respect.

"'Memory Lane'?" she asks.

I blink. "Yeah."

"God-tier sample," she says. "That organ loop? That's time travel."

Now it's me who smiles.

We sit in silence for a beat too long to be casual.

Then I ask, quietly: "You ever feel like you're doing all this right—and still somehow missing something essential?"

She doesn't answer immediately.

Then she says, "All the time. But I figure wholeness isn't something you find. It's something you remember."

She stands, smooth and certain.

"You'll be alright," she adds, soft.

Then: "But only if you let somebody else in."

And just like that—she's gone.

I don't touch the tea.

But I leave it on the desk.
Right where she placed it.
Like a reminder.

Chapter 11

"Still Not a Player"

Big Pun ft. Joe (1998)

"I'm not a player, I just crush a lot…"

I should've known better than to let the former
Faculty Association plan my love life.

But here I am.
Three dates in five weeks.
Each one less promising than the last.
Each one suggested with the same sentence:
*"She's smart, single, and owns property—what else
you need?"*

Apparently: compatibility. Timing. Actual
chemistry. Basic peace of mind.

Date One: Camille.
Sociology professor. Well-read. Wore glasses that
matched her scarf.
We met for coffee. She ordered chamomile tea,

which I didn't judge—until she used the word *"problematic"* five times before the drinks arrived.

"I just think men your age aren't honest about intimacy," she said.

"Men my age?" I asked.

"Well, you know... emotionally rigid, post-divorce, allergic to joy."

I said, "You do realize this is our first conversation, right?"

She smiled. "Exactly."

I smiled back. "You want the rest of this muffin?"

Date Two: Toni.
Kindergarten principal. Laughed easily. Wore all black like she was in mourning or retail.
Dinner was solid—until she leaned in and said, "You seem like the type still in love with someone you never even got with."

I blinked. "Damn. That's oddly specific."

She shrugged. "You flinch when you talk about women. Not in pain—just... history."

I nodded. "You an empath?"

"Yeah."

I paid the bill.
Told her I had an early morning.
She texted, "Let's be friends."

I never answered.

Date Three. I won't even name her.

We met at a wine bar.
She opened with, "So how do you feel about the multiverse and the ethics of open relationships?"

I said, "Excuse me?"

She said, "Let's skip the small talk."

She was beautiful. Brilliant. Also had no brakes.
We lasted thirty-nine minutes.

After that one, I sat in my driveway listening to
"Retrospect for Life."
Common and Lauryn whispering about missed chances and heavy love.
I sat there with the engine off, hand on the key, thinking about my patterns.

The truth is—I know exactly what the problem is.

I'm not even in the market for *new* connection.

Not really.

Because the person I'm supposed to be asking out brings me tea, hands me annotated floor plans, and knows when to leave me alone better than anyone I've ever known.

And I'm doing everything but acting on it.

Last week she said, "I like the way you protect the space but don't police it."

I said, "That's the job."

She looked at me for a beat. Not like she was impressed—but like she *wasn't buying it.*

We sat in the rec room after her workshop, just the two of us. She was packing up. I was pretending to work.

She said, "Do you ever take a breath and just… be?"

I said, "I've been trying to."

She nodded.

Then said, "Try harder."

She left me with that.

And here I am—dodging the obvious like it's gonna disappear if I ignore it long enough.

I'm not afraid of love.

I'm afraid of **messing up good peace** with clumsy timing.
Afraid of ruining a space that feels sacred with a feeling I can't control.

And maybe, deep down, I'm afraid that she already knows all this—

—and is just waiting for me to catch up.

I'm not a player.

I'm a man who overthinks.
Who stalls.
Who tells himself "maybe later" like it's a strategy and not a sentence.

But tonight, I deleted the dating app my colleague installed on my phone when I wasn't looking.

And I didn't feel bad about it.

Didn't feel like I was quitting.

Felt like I was clearing the board.

Because maybe the only move left…

is the one I keep avoiding.

Chapter 12

"Ms. Jackson"

OutKast (2000)

"I apologize a trillion times…"

I never called her Ms. Jackson.

She wouldn't have allowed it.

Her name was Rhonda Jackson when we met.
From Philly. Clear-eyed. No nonsense.
The kind of woman who said what she meant and
expected you to do the same.

We met in D.C.—when I was just starting out as a
lecturer, fresh out of grad school, still thinking
passion was the same thing as maturity. I had my
first real teaching gig, a two-bedroom apartment
with a wobbly dining table, and a head full of things
I thought I understood.

I thought knowing Baldwin and Baraka made me ready to lead.
Rhonda taught me otherwise.

She moved like clarity—career steady, values settled, schedule tight.
She didn't have time for potential dressed up in charisma.

And still… we found each other.

We weren't in love when Simone came.

We were trying.

Trying to find rhythm in a relationship built on parallel lives.
Trying to build something with two blueprints that didn't align.
Trying to parent with respect but not always understanding.

And eventually, we stopped trying.

Rhonda used to say, "I don't need a lecture. I need a partner."

But I didn't know how to be one.

I knew how to show up with a gift bag.
Knew how to plan a birthday.
Knew how to wire money on time.

But I didn't know how to stay through the boring parts.
Didn't know how to show up when it wasn't about me.

Simone's fourth birthday.
Chuck E. Cheese.
She was wearing a pink dress with light-up sneakers.
I walked in twenty-five minutes late with a remote-control truck and a battery-powered singing bear.

Rhonda pulled me aside.

"You like being the fun parent, huh?"

I shrugged. "You want me to be the bad guy?"

She said, "I want you to be **here**—when it's hard. When it's Tuesday. When she's sick. When you're tired."

I nodded. Said I'd do better.

Then missed the next school meeting.

That's the man I was.

Not cruel. Not careless.

Just unready.

Rhonda and I never fought big.
We just got quieter.
Two people managing logistics and calling it love.

Eventually, she moved back closer to her family.
Got remarried. That ended too.

Now we talk in short emails and clean texts.
Mostly about Simone.
Always cordial. Never real.

Simone never asked me why it didn't work.

She never had to.

Her eyes told me everything.

She learned early not to expect too much.
To do for herself.
To keep her questions to herself, too.

That's what hurts the most.

Not the divorce.
Not the distance.

The *conditioning*.

Last week I was driving to the grocery store when
"Ms. Jackson" came on.

That hook hit like it never had before.

*"I'm sorry Ms. Jackson, I am for real / Never meant
to make your daughter cry..."*

Used to be just a song I liked.
Now it's an indictment.

Because I know how many quiet apologies I've
made.
And how few of them I've actually said out loud.

I think that's why I've been flailing in the dating
pool.

Not because I don't want connection.

But because the last time I had a shot at something
good—
I fumbled it.

And not out of malice.

Just fear.
And pride.
And being too caught up in my own idea of "trying"
to recognize what showing up actually meant.

And now—there's someone else.

Someone who brings tea without asking.
Who sees me.
And still I haven't said anything.

Because part of me is still carrying old shame like
it's armor.

Because I'm afraid to reach for something real
when I know what I did with it last time.

Rhonda never asked for an apology.

But I owe her one anyway.

Not for what happened between us.
But for what I didn't learn soon enough.

That presence is louder than performance.
That quiet consistency is louder than charm.

I'm not sorry because of the fallout.

I'm sorry because I finally understand the lesson.

Chapter 13

"Runnin'"

The Pharcyde (1995)

"Can't keep runnin' away..."

The day is too perfect.

It's the kind of Southern spring Saturday that feels earned—like the weather finally apologized for all the cold mornings and moody wind. Seventy-two degrees. Barbecue in the air. Music playing low through half-decent speakers strung up on lamp posts. Somebody's uncle two-steppin' near the smoothie stand.

No pressure. No schedule.

She asked me to come.

"Hey, there's a community event over by the botanical garden—Black vendors, food, some art. You wanna walk?"

I said yes without even pretending to overthink it.

That was the first surprise.

We drift from booth to booth like we're in a rhythm we didn't plan.

There's a DJ playing old De La Soul, some Maxwell, even a little Amel Larrieux. No one's rushing. Kids in face paint. Women in sundresses and headwraps. People leaning into joy like it belongs to them.

And her? She's effortless. Braids pulled back, light denim jacket, sneakers that look brand new but have clearly been places.

At one booth, she hands me a candle.

"Smells like mixtape summer," she says.

I smell it. She's not wrong.

I smile. "Smells like Darius's back seat."

She laughs. "That boy stayed with a subwoofer and no gas."

And just like that—he's here again.

Memory, close behind the scent.

Not heavy. Just real.

We walk a little farther.

She's talking to a vendor about something
handmade—pillows with African print and tiny
sewn-in affirmations.

And that's when I see her.

Constance.

Across the lawn.
Standing near a tent giving away STEM kits.
She's in a yellow wrap dress, sunglasses, edges laid,
that same tall calm she always carried.
But it's the boy next to her who makes me stop.

He's older than I would've guessed.
Fourteen, maybe fifteen.
Light brown skin. Locs down to his shoulders.
Holding a basketball like it's just part of his arm.

They're laughing.

Then she looks up.

And sees me.

There's a half-second where I think I can pivot. Walk the other way. Pretend I didn't see her. Pretend I'm just here for herbal tea and plantain chips.

But she's already waving.

Already walking toward me.

"Malik?"

I try to smile. My chest is tight.

"Hey… wow."

We hug. Awkwardly. The kind of hug you give someone who used to mean something that you never named.

She pulls back, still holding my elbow lightly.

"You look good," she says.

I nod. "You too."

She turns to the boy beside her.

"This is my son, **Rodney**."

The boy nods. Polite. Quiet.

I say, "Nice to meet you."

Then she says it:

"I was hoping to run into you."

That spins me.

"Oh?"

"Yeah... **Rodney**'s been asking about a place to go after school. Something more active. And I remembered what you said about the youth center. The Spot, right?"

My throat catches.

"Yeah, The Spot."

"I looked it up. It's beautiful, Malik. I mean... it's real."

I glance at her, then him.

A kid.

A real one.

And she's here. With the son of whoever she moved on with. Maybe. I don't know. I never asked. Never could.

I swallow.

"Yeah. We'd love to have him. We do after-school stuff. Mentorship. Rec time. Real talk sessions."

Rodney looks up at me for the first time.

"You got a gym?"

I nod. "Big one."

He smirks. "Bet."

She smiles.

And it's the same smile I saw once on a porch when Darius kissed her cheek and said, *"Don't let me mess this up."*

He didn't.

Life did.

I hand her my card.

"It's all on the site, but text me directly. I'll make sure he's set."

She takes it. Brushes her thumb over the corner.

"I appreciate that."

She lingers for a beat.

Then says, "It's good to see you."

I nod.

"You too."

As she and **Rodney** walk away, I feel something between my ribs loosen and pull tight at the same time.

She doesn't look back.

And I don't blame her.

"Hey," she says, walking back to me.

The woman. The present.

She's holding two lemonades.

"Everything okay?"

I nod. "Yeah."

She studies me. Doesn't press.

Then says, "Want to go sit in the shade?"

I say yes.

But part of me is still standing in the middle of the lawn, watching the version of joy that never got to bloom walk away holding a basketball.

"Can't keep runnin' away..."

Chapter 14

"Moment of Truth"

Gang Starr (1998)

"No matter what we face, we must face the moment of truth..."

The first time Constance walks into The Spot, she does it like someone holding her breath.

Not from fear.
From memory.

The front desk greets her. The walls hum with bass. There's the smell of fresh mop water and popcorn. Kids laughing in the gym. One of the staff is playing *Midnight Marauders* in the lounge. It all feels too warm for a place built from grief.

Rodney's next to her, hoodie up, back straight. He's fifteen. Taller than I remembered. Jawline coming in. Darius' walk. Darius' quiet. That half-curious, half-cautious look like the world owes him something, but he's too proud to beg for it.

I watch them from the second-floor landing.

And in that moment, I know.
Not just suspect.

I **know**.

We greet each other, go through the motions. Show
them the building. The murals. The gym.

When we reach the tall red-and-silver panel in the
east wing, Constance pauses.

Her fingers graze it gently.

"You kept it," she says.

I nod. "I chose it because it reminded me of him."

She looks at it longer than I do. She's not seeing
paint.
She's seeing echoes.

"Yeah," she says softly. "It feels like him. Even the
silence."

Later, we sit in the empty gym—Rodney at
orientation with one of our youth leads. Constance
and I on the bleachers, space between us, but not
avoidance. Just time.

"I saw you at the event," she says. "I could tell something shifted when you looked at him."

I nod.

"I didn't ask then," I say. "But I've been wondering."

She takes a breath.
Not for drama—for clarity.

"He's Darius's."

There it is.

The truth I'd already felt in my bones.

But hearing it?
Changes everything.

"I didn't tell anyone back then," she says. "We had just started. It was new, and then... he was gone. I didn't want to make Rodney someone's memory. I wanted him to be his own person."

I nod slowly.

"Darius would've wanted to know."

"I know," she says. "And he would've shown up. I never doubted that."

She folds her hands in her lap.

"But you were part of him. You still are."

She turns to me.

"That's why I brought Rodney here. Not just because of the programs. But because I want him to know where he comes from. Who his father was. And who stood next to him."

The silence that follows isn't heavy.

It's **whole**.

Because I get it now.

The grief I've been carrying wasn't just about Darius dying.

It was about the pieces I thought were lost forever—

being right here.

That night, I find Rodney under the mural again. Sitting on the floor, back against the wall, basketball beside him.

I sit down.

"You remind me of him."

He glances at me, then nods.

"My mom said he was cool."

"He was."

"You ever think about him?"

"Every day."

Rodney looks at the panel.

Then says, "That's tight."

"Yeah," I say. "It is."

Later, I find her—the woman I still haven't named—in the event space, breaking down chairs from her workshop. She's humming something. I think it's *"Soon You'll Understand."*

"You always hum sad Jay-Z?"

She jumps. Laughs. "Only when the day's been heavy."

"You good?"

She tilts her head. "You?"

I exhale.

"Rodney's Darius's son."

She freezes for a moment, then nods.

"I figured."

"I didn't know for sure until today. But now I do."

There's a pause.

And then I say it:

"I've spent all this time trying not to let joy attach to me. Like if I kept moving, nothing could stick. But I think I've just been scared of what happens if it does."

She walks over. Sits beside me on the edge of the stage.

"You're allowed to stay still, Malik. You're allowed to be here."

And for the first time in years, I believe that might be true.

Chapter 15

"I Used to Love H.E.R."

Common (1994)

"I met this girl when I was ten years old / And what I loved most, she had so much soul..."

The first time I heard *"I Used to Love H.E.R."*, I was at Darius's place, sitting cross-legged on the floor next to a milk crate full of CDs.

He slid the disc in, looked at me with that grin he got when he knew something was about to hit different, and said:
"Just listen."

So I did.

And I remember being still for the whole song.
No jokes. No side commentary.
Just still.

Because it didn't sound like a love song at first.

But it was.

It was about change.

About watching someone—or something—you loved transform into something you couldn't always recognize.

It was about **grief disguised as nostalgia.**

"Now I see her in commercials / She's universal…"

That line stuck with me for years. Still does.

Because I've seen it happen, too.

Hip hop started as home. As truth. As survival. As joy.

She raised me.

She gave me my language, my rhythm, my armor.

But somewhere along the way, she started showing up in packages I didn't trust.
Remixed. Marketed. Watered down.

And I still loved her.

But not the same way.

Now, years later, I think about her every time I stand inside The Spot, watching a group of kids throw on *Earl Sweatshirt* and *Cordae* and argue about who's underrated.

They've never heard *The Low End Theory* front to back.

But they love her. In their way.

And that's what matters.

She's still alive.

And then there's **Alexis**.

I haven't said her name in these pages yet.

Not because I forgot it.

Because I wasn't ready.

I sat with her in my office this morning. She brought coffee without asking. Mine had cinnamon in it. Somehow, she just knew.

We didn't talk much. She asked about Rodney. I asked about her urban planning workshop and how she got that quiet group of teenagers to open up.

She smiled and said, "Silence makes room for truth."

I didn't respond.

Because it felt like that sentence had been aimed at my chest.

She's not flashy. Not performative. She doesn't walk into rooms expecting the light to shift. But somehow, it always does.

She asks hard questions with soft eyes.
Stays just long enough to be felt.
Leaves just before I get too comfortable.

She's careful with people.

And I realize now—she's been careful with me.

There was a moment, a few weeks back, when she adjusted a frame on the wall in the east hallway and said, "You always curate the energy in here on purpose, don't you?"

I said, "It's not just a space. It's a system."

She nodded like she understood what I meant, even though I wasn't sure I did.

The way I used to love hip hop is the way I'm starting to feel about her.

Like I knew her before I met her.

Like I've spent years mourning something I didn't think I'd ever find again.

And now she's here—not asking to be chased, not asking to be defined.

Just *present*.

Late that night, I'm locking up The Spot.

The place is quiet. Everyone's gone. The last door clicks shut behind me, and I do what I always do: take one slow lap before I leave.

I walk past the main mural, past the rec room, and stop in front of the red and silver panel in the east hallway.

It's always been the loudest quiet in the building.

Where I feel Darius most.

Not in some ghostly way.

More like... weight.

Like he's holding the place up from the inside.

I stand there, keys in hand, and say it softly—barely
more than a whisper.

"Her name is Alexis."

I've known it since she introduced herself.

But this is the first time I've said it **here**.
In this space.
To *him*.

And it feels like saying it makes it real.

Like it means I've finally let it in.

I stare at the panel a little longer.

Then I say:

"I think I'm still in love."

Not with her only.
Not with hip hop only.
But with **life**, in a way I haven't been in a long time.

And for once, I don't flinch when I hear myself say
it.

Chapter 16

"God Lives Through"

A Tribe Called Quest (1993)

"Act like you know, not now, but right now..."

It wasn't a day full of fireworks. No emotional avalanche. Just a normal Tuesday that carried a different kind of weight.

The Spot was calm by the evening—kids gone, volunteers cleaning up, somebody playing *Camp Lo* low on a Bluetooth speaker in the corner.

By the time I locked the front door, the sky was already inked out and the building had that quiet hum it only gets when it's been full of people all day and suddenly remembers it's made of walls again.

I stayed late.

Not because I had to.

Because something in me needed the stillness.

I sat in my office with the lights off, letting the blue tint from the streetlight smear across the desk.

I thought about Darius. About that crooked smile that made everything sound like a plan, even when it wasn't.

I thought about Rodney, and the way he's been showing up—more often, more present, asking real questions. The way his voice cracked when he asked if I thought Darius would've liked him.

I thought about Alexis, and how her silence carries more understanding than most people's advice.

And then I picked up the phone.

Gerald answered on the second ring.

That was rare.

He usually lets it ring all the way out just to call me back and say he "missed it by a second."

"Malik," he said.

"Hey, Pop."

His voice wasn't sharp, wasn't soft. Just there.

"I figured I owed you a real conversation."

"You don't owe me anything," he said, and for once, it didn't sound defensive. Just matter-of-fact.

"I know. That's why I'm calling."

I told him about Darius. About how it still hurts more than I admit. About how some days, I walk through The Spot and expect him to be in the next room.

I told him about Constance. About Rodney. That he's fifteen now. Smart. Reserved. The kind of kid who's already carrying questions too big for his age.

I told him the truth I'd never said out loud to him:

"That kid's Darius's son. And I didn't know until she brought him to me. Not really. But I see it in him every time he walks in the building."

There was silence on the line. I could hear tools clinking faintly in the background, like he was fixing something just to keep his hands busy.

And then I said it:

"And there's someone else. Her name's Alexis."

I waited for the weight to shift.

For the old man sigh or the guarded redirect.

But it didn't come.

Instead, he said, "Tell me about her."

So I did.

Told him how she doesn't fill the room with noise, but somehow rearranges the space just by being in it. How she listens harder than anyone I've ever met. How she challenges me without making me feel smaller.

How I've been afraid to name it because the last time I did, I lost more than I could carry.

"I didn't know how to talk about things," he said after a pause. "When your mother passed, I shut it all down. Thought silence was strength. Turns out it's just… quiet."

I let the words sit.

Then he added, "But I've always been proud of you. Even when I didn't say it. Especially then."

My chest went tight in a way I wasn't ready for.

"You're not late, Pop."

"I hope not," he said.

After we hung up, I sat there for a while, phone in my lap, staring at the dim reflection of my own face in the window.

Then I hit Simone's name on my favorites list.

She answered halfway through the second ring, bonnet on, eating cereal like it was dinner.

"Hey, Dad."

"Hey. What you eating?"

"Business."

We talked about her students. How one of them lied about having a peanut allergy to get out of class. How she's thinking about teaching summer enrichment instead of taking time off.

She's grown. And I still forget sometimes that she knows me.

Really knows me.

"You ever think I hold back too much?" I asked.

She raised an eyebrow. "You mean emotionally or just in general?"

"Both."

She gave me that smirk she got from her mother—half kind, half cutting.

"Dad… you love hard. You just ration it. Like there's a shortage."

I laughed.

Then she looked at me, a little quieter. A little more precise.

"There's someone, right?"

I didn't answer right away.

She leaned in closer on the screen.

"Say it to me out loud, Dad. Her name."

I swallowed.

Then said, "Alexis."

And when I said it, something settled in my chest.

Not weight.

Root.

She smiled.

"There it is."

After we hung up, I didn't turn the lights on.

I just walked out of the office, back into the empty
hallway, and stood beneath the red and silver panel.

The one that reminds me of movement. Of rhythm.
Of fire held still.

I pulled up my playlist and tapped on one track.

The one that never leaves the rotation.

"God Lives Through."

The speakers filled the room.

"Act like you know, not now, but right now…"

I let it play through once.

Then again.

And somewhere between the first verse and the last hook, I closed my eyes and said softly:

"Thank you."

I don't know who I was talking to.

Maybe Darius.
Maybe God.
Maybe myself.

But I meant it.

Chapter 17

"The Blast"

Talib Kweli & Hi-Tek (2000)

"Sometimes it's far and between, I'm sad to say / It got my brain crowded like sunset on a Saturday"

I moved different the next morning.

Didn't plan to. Didn't write a mantra or do a breathing ritual.

I just... *was.*

Lighter, maybe. But not soft.

Like someone who'd finally laid down a bag he didn't even know he was carrying through security every day.

The Spot was already moving by the time I got there—kids in the lounge talking over each other, a volunteer wheeling in juice boxes for the fridge, someone sweeping near the front.

But it didn't feel chaotic. It felt **alive**.

It felt like the building had finally caught its own rhythm.

Rodney was in the gym early—ball under one arm, hoodie half-zipped, one earbud in.

I nodded at him. He gave me the chin-lift that meant *we're good.*

I watched him shoot for a minute. His form is clean. No wasted motion. And he's got that Darius thing— he drifts a little after each shot, like he's already on his way to the next thing.

And yeah—he's good.

But I'm already thinking I'll need to work with him a little.

Because **I was always the better hooper between me and his dad**, and I'm not about to let the record get rewritten without a little coaching.

On the way to the rec room, I passed Alexis in the main hallway. She was carrying two boxes of workshop materials and a clipboard tucked under her arm.

"Morning," she said.

I said it back.

Then stopped. Turned.

"Need help?"

She raised an eyebrow, smiled lightly.

"You offering, or fishing for praise?"

"Little of both," I said.

She shook her head and handed me one of the boxes.

"Come on."

We walked in silence, and it was the kind that's earned—not awkward, just clean. Like we'd moved past needing to fill the space.

When we got to her room, I followed her in, set the box down on the table, and hesitated.

"Can I ask you something?" I said.

She didn't look up from her clipboard.

"You just did."

I smiled. "You ever feel like things are speeding up, but finally making sense?"

Now she looked up.

"That means you're paying attention."

I nodded.

"You make this place better."

She didn't miss a beat.

"So do you."

Back in my office, I caught Rodney slipping something into the feedback box we keep in the hallway. He didn't see me.

After he walked off, I pulled it out.

It was a list.

No name. Just four lines:

1. How do you stop missing people?
2. Is it okay to still be mad?
3. Do dreams count if they're not realistic?
4. What would he have said to me?

I folded it slowly and sat with it.

Didn't rush to answer.
Didn't toss it either.

Just... kept it close.

Later that day, I passed Rodney again in the hallway
near the gym. He was sipping from a water bottle,
hoodie sleeves pushed to his elbows.

He nodded at me. I nodded back.

Then, right as I passed him, he said:

"You move different when she's around."

I stopped.

"What's that?"

He leaned back against the wall.

Grinned just a little—only on one side, like he was
testing a joke before he committed to it.

"She got your rhythm doing something new. That
ain't nothing to play with."

And right there—

I heard Darius.

Clear as day.

It took me back. Not to anything recent—but to *way back.*

College days. Sophomore year, maybe. I'd been caught up over somebody I wasn't ready to admit I cared about.

Darius had leaned against the hood of my **old Corolla**, eyes low, smile cocked to the side.

"That ain't nothing to play with, bruh."

Same phrasing.
Same grin.
Same truth spoken without ceremony.

Rodney didn't know he was echoing his father.

But I knew.

And for a second, I wasn't just remembering Darius.

I was *hearing* him—through his son.

Later, Simone texted me a photo of her and her students at a community garden.

Underneath it, she wrote:

You're doing alright, old man.

I smiled. Saved the photo. Let myself feel all of it.

Everything's still messy.

Grief still shows up unannounced.
The past still sings some nights when I don't want it
to.

But now?

The music doesn't scare me.

Chapter 18

"You Got Me"

The Roots ft. Erykah Badu (1999)

"If you were worried 'bout where / I been or who I saw or / What club I went to with my homies / Baby don't worry, you know that you got me""

It started with a power outage.

Not dramatic. Just a flicker, then dark.

The Spot had closed for the night, but Alexis was still upstairs finishing something for the urban planning cohort, and I was downstairs restocking the rec room fridge.

One second I was stacking Gatorades.

Next, I was standing in the dim, emergency red glow of an exit sign, holding a lemon-lime like it was going to explain something.

Outside, thunder rolled—not the sharp kind, the kind that sounds like someone dragging a couch across the sky. Rain tapped the windows in rhythm.

I called up the stairs.

"You good?"

"Yeah," she called back. "I think the storm tripped the box. I've got my phone light. You?"

"All good down here."

Bet.
Then: "You want to come up?"

By the time I reached the second floor, she had already pulled two chairs into the open space just outside the workshop room.

Her phone light was wedged into a mason jar, casting a soft, uneven glow up the wall.

Window cracked just enough to hear the storm. Smelled like concrete and summer air.

She looked up when I stepped in and patted the second chair.

"Sit," she said.

So I did.

We sat like that for a minute.
Two, maybe more.

I could feel her presence—not just next to me, but around me.

She didn't need to fill the space.
She let it *breathe*.

"You remember that Roots song?" I said eventually.

She smirked. Didn't even need the name.

"You Got Me."

I nodded. "Played it to death junior year."

"Of course you did," she said. "Every college dude with a stereo and a window view did."

I laughed. "You're not wrong."

She leaned back in her chair a little, arms crossed, eyes watching the rain. "I used to skip to the part where Erykah comes in. That's when it got real."

"That's what made it feel like love," I said. "Not just the bars. Her voice. Like the part of the relationship you don't brag about."

She glanced at me. "The quiet part."

"Exactly."

I let the silence settle again.

She didn't reach to break it. That's one of the things I respect about her—she's not afraid of what silence might say.

"I used to think that song was just about loyalty," I said eventually. "Like… don't cheat, don't lie, don't flinch."

"And now?"

I looked at her.

"Now I think it's about presence. About not leaving when it's easier to disappear. It's about standing in a storm and not checking your watch."

She held my gaze.

"That's what I've always wanted," she said. "Not the show. Not the story. Just the *proof.*"

I sat with that for a second.

Her voice was soft, but it didn't waver.

I thought about every time I'd started to drift away
from joy because I didn't trust it to stay.
About how I used to think protection meant
distance.
About how Alexis never asked me to chase
anything—just to **be here**.

"You've been good to me," I said finally. "And I've
been slow about saying it. But I see you, Alexis. I
really do."

She smiled, but not a flashy one.
The kind that lets you know a wall has quietly come
down.

"I see you too, Malik."

Thunder cracked again, closer this time.

The lights stayed off.

Neither of us moved.

We just sat in the flicker, letting truth be its own
kind of light.

It wasn't a kiss.
It didn't need to be.

It was a shift.

The kind you feel in your chest and your fingertips
and the back of your throat.

A moment that doesn't rush to be named.

A little while later, I walked her out to her car with
an umbrella. She unlocked the door but didn't get in
right away.

"You good?" I asked.

"I am," she said. "And I think you are too."

I nodded.

And this time, I didn't second-guess it.

Chapter 19

"Love Is"

Common (2005)

"How beautiful love can be / On the streets love is hard to see / It's a place I got to be / Loving you is loving me"

There's something about making breakfast that tells the truth about your spirit.

That morning, I cracked eggs with a rhythm I hadn't felt in a while. Pan sizzling, kettle humming behind me. "Electric Relaxation" low on my phone, floating between memory and now.

Not background music—**mood music**.

There wasn't a voice in my head second-guessing the day. No need to rehearse every move.
Just breath.
Just ease.

I was meeting Alexis for lunch later—nothing fancy. A café near the university. The kind of place where the lighting is soft and nobody's in a rush to leave. I'd texted her late the night before, after she got home, just one line:

Let's stop waiting to feel ready. Let's just be.

She replied:

Yes.

Before that, I swung by The Spot. Saturdays move slower, but there's still rhythm—basketball practice, a quiet tutoring session in Room 4, a group of teens piecing together a short film project that was turning into something real.

Rodney was in the mural hallway. Alone. Studying the panel like it might change if he stared long enough.

I walked over.

"Hey."

He didn't flinch.

"Yo."

We stood in silence for a second. Then I said, "You thinking or listening?"

"Both," he said. "Sometimes I think about what it means to be from someone I don't remember."

I nodded. Let him speak.

"I asked Coach if I could help out next season. With the younger kids."

"That's good," I said. "You'd be great at that."

He looked back at the mural again.

"You know... I've been mad at him for a long time."

"I know."

"And I think I was more mad that I didn't get a chance to know him. Mad at time. Mad at the whole situation."

I waited.

Then said, "You still can, in some ways."

He glanced at me, quieter this time.

"You think I got him in me?"

I smiled.

"Every time you talk with your eyes first."

He didn't smile, but he didn't need to. That landed.

On my way out, I passed Constance in the main entrance, talking to one of the volunteers. She saw me and nodded toward the hallway.

"He okay?"

"He's finding his own way in."

She exhaled, steady.

"I see him opening up more around you," she said.

I leaned against the wall. "I'm not trying to take anything from him. Or from you."

"I know that," she said. "And he does too."

She paused.

"I just want him to have people who don't flinch."

We looked at each other for a long second. No past to unpack. Just now.

"You're part of the village, Malik. Whether you meant to be or not."

Lunch with Alexis felt like something familiar but new—like finding your favorite hoodie after thinking you lost it in a move.

We sat by the window. She wore a deep green sweater and that smile that always looked like it knew more than it was letting on.

"Thanks for making time," I said.

"I didn't make it," she said. "I had it."

We talked about everything and nothing. The city's zoning policies. Her playlist rotation. My stubborn left knee.

I told her about Rodney's moment at the mural.

She listened all the way through, eyes never leaving mine.

"That's what love looks like," she said. "When you don't rush the healing."

As we were walking back to our cars, I asked if she had time to swing by The Spot with me. She didn't hesitate.

Rodney was still there—now helping break down folding chairs from a youth meeting.

He looked up when we walked in, wiped his hands on his hoodie.

"Hey," he said.

Alexis offered a small smile.

"I heard you've been coaching."

He shrugged. "Trying."

"You're not trying," I said. "You're doing."

She glanced at me, then back at him. "That's how it starts."

He didn't say much, but his posture shifted. Just a little.

The three of us didn't talk long. But it felt like something small clicked into place.

That night, I stood in the mirror longer than usual.

Not because I didn't recognize myself.

But because I finally did.

Chapter 20

"93 'Til Infinity"

Souls of Mischief (1993)

"Exchangin' facts about impacts, 'cause in facts / My freestyle talent overpowers, brothers can't hack it"

There's something about the smell of charcoal and the sound of basketballs echoing in a half-full gym that makes you feel like the world is *still trying to get it right.*

The Spot's first community cookout wasn't anything fancy. No hashtags. No city funding. Just grills, music, folding tables, a few coolers, and a neighborhood that needed a reason to stay awhile.

We set up early. Alexis in joggers, hair in two thick braids, sliding boxes of bottled water under a table like she'd done this a thousand times.

Rodney helped with the sound check, grumbling as he tried to untangle a mess of speaker cables. I walked over with a flash drive in my hand.

"I want to show you something," I said.

He raised an eyebrow. "This ain't gonna be one of those 'back in my day' speeches, is it?"

"Nah," I said, smiling. "This one's deeper than that."

I plugged it in, queued up the track, and let the beat ride for a second before the lyrics even came in.

Then came the intro:

"Yo, what's up? This is Tajai of the mighty Souls of Mischief crew / I'm chillin' with my man Phesto, my man A-Plus / And my man Op', you know he's dope."

Rodney cocked his head at the speaker.

"This was your dad's favorite song," I said.

He turned toward the sound, arms crossed, like he wasn't ready for what it might stir.

"He used to play this in his car like it was scripture. Said it made him feel like he could float."

Rodney didn't speak.

He just nodded and listened.

The beat settled in, that laid-back Bay Area swing. The hook hit:

"This is how we chill from '93 'til..."

Rodney tapped one foot, eyes lowered. But I saw it.

He wasn't just hearing it.

He was *taking it in.*

The grill started up slow. I was on burger duty while Alexis handled the drinks and registration table. Simone surprised me by showing up right before noon, shades on, curls popping, and that walk that said, *Don't act like you didn't miss me.*

"I see you made it."

"I told you I would," she said. "Also, free food."

We hugged longer than usual.

"You good?"

"I am," she said. "You look it, too."

Simone and Alexis spent time near the folding tables, talking like they'd known each other longer than they had. Watching them from the grill felt like seeing two parts of my life actually sit down at the same table. No tension. No decoding. Just women who cared about me, finding room for each other.

Rodney got into a two-on-two game with the younger kids. He coached more than played, calling out picks, clapping when somebody got a shot off clean. When one of the smaller kids tripped and skinned his knee, Rodney helped him up, patted his back, and said, "You alright. Get back in."

That right there?

That was Darius.

Not just the tone. The **timing.**

Later, *"93 'Til Infinity"* played again—this time coming from the main speaker, bouncing off the walls of The Spot and out into the crowd.

I was standing near the grill, spatula in hand, when that line came on:

"Exchangin' facts about impacts, 'cause in facts / My freestyle talent overpowers, brothers can't hack it."

I closed my eyes for a second.

Because that was me now.
Not performing.
Not explaining.
Just flowing.

In my rhythm.

In my purpose.

Constance approached me with a paper plate in one hand and sweet tea in the other.

"He's lighter," she said.

"Yeah," I nodded. "He is."

She looked at me.

"So are you."

I exhaled.

"Today feels good."

"It feels earned," she said.

As the sun started leaning into the sidewalk, the music still pulsing low, Alexis came up beside me with a plate of grilled pineapple and two lemonades.

"This was good," she said.

"This was necessary," I replied.

We stood like that, not saying much, watching The Spot **become exactly what it was supposed to be.**

Not an idea.
Not a project.
Not a dream deferred.

Just... **real.**

Rodney walked past us, headed toward the tables. As he passed, he looked at me and said, "That song?"

I raised my eyebrows.

"It's got that bounce to it," he said. "I get why he loved it."

Then he jogged off.

And I stood there a moment longer, feeling that bounce in my chest, like maybe Malik-from-back-then would've been proud of Malik-from-right-now.

Chapter 21

"Rewind"

Nas (2001)

"Listen up gangstas and honeys with your hair done / Pull up a chair, hon' and put it in the air, son..."

We were sitting on the couch, her feet tucked beneath her, a blanket draped across her lap like she was in her own living room—even though it was mine.

The rain outside had slowed to a whisper. The lights were low. My playlist was playing something warm but wordless—horns and keys, nothing too on-the-nose.

We'd been talking about Rodney. About how he'd been more open, more present. I told her about how I'd caught him rapping quietly along to "93 'Til Infinity" earlier that week and how he smiled when he thought nobody saw.

She said, "That's when they're starting to come into themselves. When they stop performing and start just being."

And then she asked:

"So... tell me about Simone's mom."

She didn't ask like she was checking boxes.

She asked like she was making space.

Like she already knew there was something *unfinished* in the way I'd mentioned Rhonda before, but didn't press for it then.

I took a deep breath.

"We were young when we got married. Twenty-four. Both of us working jobs that felt bigger than we were ready for. She had ambition, and so did I— but mine kept turning into something sharper. Like I had something to prove."

"Was it love?" she asked.

"It was," I said. "And it was also pride. And survival. And ego. And fear. We didn't know how to say 'I'm scared' without making it sound like a threat."

Alexis didn't respond right away.

She just folded her arms and tucked her legs in closer. Not retreating. Just... listening.

I looked at the coffee table, at the sweat ring from her tea mug and the quiet reflection of the light above us.

"She was a good mother. Still is. And I didn't make it easy. I was obsessed with control. With order. I thought discipline and stability were enough to make a relationship work. I kept thinking if I provided enough, she'd feel safe. But I wasn't *available*."

I paused.

"I missed anniversaries. I missed doctor's appointments. I even missed a parent-teacher conference once—Simone's first one in kindergarten. Rhonda didn't yell. She didn't even raise her voice. She just... looked at me like I had no idea what I was choosing."

Alexis blinked slowly. "And did you?"

"Not at the time."

I swallowed.

"But I do now."

She set her mug down gently.

"Have you ever told her that?"

I shook my head. "No. Not like this. I said the generic stuff. The 'sorry you feel that way' kind of stuff. The 'I was doing my best' speech. But I never really told her *my truth*."

"And now?"

"I think I want to. Not to fix the past. Just... to stop dragging it."

She nodded. "You don't owe her closure. But if you feel like you're still holding it... maybe you owe yourself the peace."

The silence between us then wasn't awkward.

It was sacred.

The kind of silence you earn when someone sees you and doesn't look away.

I leaned forward and rubbed my palms together, warming myself against something internal.

"She gave me grace longer than she should have," I said. "And when she stopped, I blamed her for walking away. But now, I get it. She didn't walk away from me. She walked toward *herself.* And that's something I can respect now."

Alexis touched my knee, just enough for me to feel her hand, then let it rest there.

"And Simone?" she asked.

"That's what keeps me thinking about it. I want her to know... I want her to see that growth isn't just in how you parent—it's in how you repair."

Later that night, after Alexis went home, I stood in the hallway holding my phone, staring at Rhonda's number. I didn't call.

But I did something I hadn't done in years.

I opened a blank message and just started typing.

Not to send.
Not yet.
But to say it out loud.

Rhonda—
I know this is out of nowhere, but I wanted to tell
you something I should've said a long time ago. I
was wrong. Not just in the ways you already know,
but in the ways I never had the courage to admit.
You asked me to show up, and I made showing up
look like presence when I was really hiding in plain
sight.
You deserved better.
And I hope this doesn't make your day harder. I just
needed you to know—I see it now.

I saved it.

Didn't delete it.

Didn't send it.

Not yet.

But it's there now.

Waiting.

Before I turned in, Simone texted me. A photo of a student's drawing, wild and bright. The kind of kid art that doesn't care about clean lines or perfect shading.

A self-portrait with a speech bubble that said:

"I'm good at not quitting."

Underneath, she wrote:

My class made these for our self-worth wall. Thought you'd like this one.

And I did.

Because for the first time in a long time, I wasn't just living forward.

I was *rewinding with purpose.*

Chapter 22

"I Wonder"

Kanye West (2007)

"And I wonder / If you know / What it means / To find your dreams..."

There's a certain quiet that only exists before the city fully wakes up.

Not silence—just the *absence* of noise.

I'd started walking again in the mornings. No destination, no steps goal, no training app chirping in my ear. Just walking. Being. Moving through my thoughts like I was flipping through old vinyl— some tracks I didn't want to replay, others I hadn't heard clearly the first time.

That morning, the air felt like a question.

And I had no answers.
But I showed up anyway.

I took the long route—past the high school, through the park trail behind the library, across the cracked sidewalk that used to run in front of the old gas station where me and Darius would meet after class to freestyle and talk mess.

Now it was a juice bar.

I didn't hate it.

Just... **missed something.**

In my head, the beat from Kanye's *"I Wonder"* looped quietly.

Not blaring.
Not demanding attention.

Just there, like a soundtrack to a chapter I didn't realize I was writing.

I hadn't sent the message to Rhonda.

It was still sitting in my drafts. Not mocking me. Just... watching. Like it was saying, *You know what needs to happen. I'm here when you're ready.*

And I kept hearing Alexis's voice in my head:

"Maybe you owe yourself the peace."

Back home, I made coffee and sat with a yellow legal pad I hadn't touched in over a year. There was something about handwriting that felt more honest. No autocorrect. No delete key. Just you, the ink, and whatever spilled out.

I wrote:

What would I say to the man I used to be—if he walked into this room right now?

Do I want to be forgiven—or just understood?

What would it take to fully show up for Simone, no matter what version of me she's already memorized?

I thought about Simone at twelve—standing in the doorway after I missed another school play.

She didn't cry. She just looked at me with that same restraint I used to carry as a kid when my dad said he was "on the way" and didn't show.

That look like: *I know you love me, but I don't know if you know how to prove it.*

And that's the part that still breaks me open
sometimes.

Because she never threw it back at me in anger.
She just adapted.

And now she's this incredible woman—soft-
spoken, strong, silly, guarded. Teaching kids how to
name their value. And I wonder...
**Did she ever stop waiting for me to show up
differently?**

Alexis called mid-morning.

"Did I catch you in the middle of something?"

"Just wondering," I said.

She laughed lightly. "That's a good place to be.
Most people stay stuck avoiding it."

I told her about my walk.
About the legal pad.
About the memory of Simone at twelve.

She didn't say, *You were doing your best.*
She didn't say, *You're being too hard on yourself.*

She just said:

"Sounds like you're finally seeing it from the outside. And from the inside."

We didn't stay on the phone long. She had a site visit. I had a life to keep building.

But before we hung up, I asked:

"You got time to walk later?"

"I always got time for that," she said.

And there it was again.

Not a declaration.
Not a demand.

Just **space**.
Offered freely.

And the question behind it:

Can I be whole and still be loved?

Chapter 23

"1nce Again"

A Tribe Called Quest (1996)

"Ohhhh, you did it to me 1nce Again my friend / I swear you do it to me every time / 'Cause you stay crazy on my mind…"

I flew into Tampa early Friday morning. Just one bag. No distractions. No expectations other than to be present.

Simone was being honored—Educator of the Year. First Black woman under 35 to receive it at her school in over a decade. She'd only told me because I asked what she had going on.

"There's this thing," she said. "No pressure. But I'd love it if you came."

That's how she does things—light touch, big meaning.

So I came.

Alexis didn't ask to come with me.
Didn't ask if I needed backup.

She just looked at me across the kitchen table that morning and said:

"This is your moment. I'm with you anyway."

I'd never had someone say less and mean more.

The ceremony was held at a polished cultural arts center—glass walls, soft jazz, name tags, pride wrapped in catered hors d'oeuvres.

I arrived early. Wanted a moment to find my seat, to get settled.

Third row, left side.

Rhonda was already there, sitting with the quiet posture of someone who wasn't waiting for anything—just **witnessing**.

We made eye contact. She gave me a nod. Not an invitation. Not resistance. Just acknowledgment.

And for once, I didn't need more than that.

Simone stepped on stage halfway through the program—calm, radiant, composed in that way I never was at her age. White blouse, gold hoops, a presence that didn't ask for attention but held it anyway.

When they introduced her, I clapped like I hadn't heard the name before. Like I wasn't still learning how to say it with the pride she deserved.

She spoke without looking at her notes.

She thanked her students first. Her principal. Her co-teachers. Her mother.

Then she paused.

"And my father is here today."

My spine went straight.

"I appreciate you being here. And for how you're showing up."

That was it.

And that was **everything**.

After the ceremony, people swirled around her like petals in soft wind—colleagues, mentors, old classmates. I waited at the edge of the room until the crowd thinned and her eyes finally found mine.

"Hey," I said.

"Hey," she smiled.

"You crushed that."

"I know."

We both laughed. Mine broke first.

I handed her a bouquet—sunflowers and greenery, simple, no fluff.

"Not sure if you like these."

"I love them," she said, taking them carefully. "Mom always got these when she had good news."

"Felt right, then."

We stepped off to the side, toward a small corridor near the exit. Just the two of us.

"You looked like yourself up there," I said. "Not the version of you trying to be impressive. Just... you."

"That's what I was going for."

I nodded. "You've become something real. I hope you know that."

"I do," she said.

Then, softer: "And I see you trying to be real, too. That means more than you know."

I looked at her for a second longer than I had before. And I saw it—not just her growth, but her *grace.*

She could've shut me out years ago. Could've chosen cold distance. But she didn't. She left the door cracked, just enough for me to find my way back.

"I know I wasn't always the version of myself you needed," I said, voice low.

Simone didn't flinch.

"But you're here now," she said. "And it's not just today."

She took a breath. "You feel different. Calmer. Like... you're listening more."

"I am."

She reached out and touched my wrist—light, like she was checking to see if the pulse underneath was real.

"Don't lose this," she said. "Don't let this be a one-time thing."

"I won't."

"I'm still learning how to trust that."

"I know. And I'll keep earning it."

She nodded slowly.

"That's all I needed to hear."

Rhonda approached me later, near the elevator.

She stood like someone who had something to say and had already decided not to sugarcoat it.

"You good?" she asked.

"I think I'm getting there."

She gave a small nod.

"I read the message."

"I figured."

"I didn't reply because I didn't want to say something I didn't mean. But now I think I can."

I stood still, let the space open up.

"I forgave you. Not recently. A while ago. But I kept holding on to the weight anyway. I didn't know how to let go without feeling like it erased what happened."

I swallowed. "It doesn't."

"I know," she said. "And neither does forgiveness."

She looked me dead in the eye.

"But what you said? It mattered. And what you did today? That mattered too."

I nodded. "I never wanted to erase the past. I just wanted to finally face it."

"We both did."

No hug. Just truth.

And then: "Simone's proud of you. You can tell, right?"

"I can now."

"Then don't mess it up."

Back at the hotel, I sat by the window barefoot, lights off, watching the streetlamps flicker down into pools of amber across the street.

For the first time in a long time, I didn't feel like I was chasing some version of myself I never got to become.

I felt **here**.

Whole.

Present.

I pulled out my phone and opened my message thread with Alexis.

Today felt like something old I finally put down.

She wrote back almost immediately:

Proud of you. Come back whole.

And I realized something:

I already had.

Chapter 24

"We Fight/We Love"

Q-Tip (2008)

"He squints, he thinks he starts to sigh / Sometimes he cry / When he think about his girlfriend on his side / She held him down, she made him better"

It started small.

A text.

"We still good for tonight?"

I stared at it longer than I should have. Not because I didn't want to see her. But because I wasn't sure *who* I'd be when she walked through the door.

Two days back from Tampa and I still hadn't exhaled completely. The things that happened—Simone's voice at the podium, Rhonda's calm forgiveness, that feeling of being both seen and unburdened for the first time in years—they hadn't left me.

But I hadn't made room for them either.

They just… sat there. On my chest. On the back of my tongue.

Alexis came by just before six.

She didn't come dressed to impress. No heels. No earrings. Just her—sweats, scarf, hoodie. But the way she looked at me?
Like she was reading past what I said before I even spoke.

I handed her a plate. She smiled. "Thai again?"

"You said you liked it last time."

"I do. I like that you remembered."

She sat down and took a sip of water, watching me like she was waiting for the air to shift.

We ate in near-silence.

Then she said it, mid-bite:

"You've been quiet."

"I've just been thinking."

"You do that when you're holding something back."

It wasn't an accusation.
It wasn't even heavy.

It was a sentence placed gently between us—like a bridge she was willing to walk halfway across if I'd meet her there.

I looked down at my food, then back at her.

"It's not about hiding. It's just... hard to translate the past when you're still trying to make sense of the present."

She nodded, slowly. "I don't need a breakdown. I need honesty."

That's when something cracked in me. Quietly. No dramatics. Just... a shift.

I set my fork down, pushed the plate aside.

"I haven't cried since I got back. But I've wanted to. More than once. In the hotel. On the plane. Last night, even."

She looked at me—not surprised. Not shaken.

Just **open**.

"And?"

"I couldn't. Something in me still holds that too tightly."

She reached across the table. Took my hand, thumb rubbing gently across my skin.

"Let it go when you're ready. I'm not keeping score."

I nodded, throat tight.

We moved to the couch, slow, like the moment needed time to carry itself.

She curled into me, legs tucked, one hand resting on my chest.

I exhaled.

Finally.

"You know what's wild?" I said after a few minutes. "I kept thinking of you while I was with Rhonda."

She looked up slightly. "Yeah?"

"Not in comparison. Just… the contrast. Rhonda loved me when I was trying to prove I was a man. You love me while I'm learning *how* to be one."

She didn't say anything. Just rested her head against me again.

"I thought vulnerability meant weakness," I said. "Like if I let someone see me undone, they'd stop seeing me at all. But you…"

I paused.

"You just hold the pieces without asking me to hurry up and fix them."

She whispered, "That's love, Malik."

I sat with that.

Let it land.

And then, almost to myself, I said:

"He squints, he thinks he starts to sigh / Sometimes he cry / When he think about his girlfriend on his side / She held him down, she made him better."

She smiled. "Q-Tip really said it all, huh?"

"Yeah," I said. "He did."

We stayed like that for a long time.

No TV. No playlist. No noise.

Just **presence**.

No performance. No fixing. Just two people who understood that *fighting* didn't always mean conflict. Sometimes it meant **staying in the room**.

Later that night, the room felt different.

Still quiet. Still low-lit. Still full of unsaid things.

But something had opened between us.

The space between her hand and mine wasn't just comfort anymore—it was invitation. Not for answers. Not for closure.

Just… **presence**. Full and unguarded.

She touched my face like it was something worth remembering.
I traced her jaw like I was learning a language I'd always heard but never spoken fluently.

No rush.
No performance.
Just time.

Given freely. Received fully.

At one point, we both exhaled at the same time.

And neither of us filled the silence that followed.

Because it was enough.

Because *we* were enough.

After, we lay there—her fingers still tracing the edge of my shoulder, my hand wrapped loosely around her waist.

No words.

Just breath and warmth and the soft comfort of **mutual knowing**.

She whispered, "You still thinking?"

"A little."

"What about?"

"That I never knew love could feel like… this."

She smiled into the curve of my neck.

"Now you do."

Chapter 25

The Map

The morning air held a kind of warmth that made everything feel easy.

The trees leaned a little less heavy. The sidewalks didn't feel rushed. Even the cars seemed to be taking their time.

I walked to The Spot without music, just me and the soft hum of the neighborhood. The thud of a basketball somewhere. A dog barking two streets over. The breeze folding itself around my thoughts.

For once, I wasn't planning.

Wasn't replaying.

Just walking.

Simone had texted me earlier that morning.

"One of my kids called me 'Mrs. Hope' today. I didn't correct him."

Underneath: a picture of her student holding a homemade certificate made of crayon and ambition.

I smiled, my chest full.

Not just because of her.

Because I was here to receive the moment. **Present.** Not waiting to be told what it meant. Just feeling it.

The Spot looked like it always did—unpolished, real, sacred.

Inside, Rodney was already there, hunched over a panel near the far wall. Hoodie, headphones, brush in hand, sketchbook open beside him. Focused.

"Yo," he said, without looking up.

"You beat me here?"

"I was up."

"You good?"

"Yeah," he said. "Just had stuff I needed to get out."

"You ever sleep?"

"Sometimes," he grinned.

He pointed to the panel he was working on. A pair of open hands, palms up, with fragments of color rising from them like smoke or stories.

Underneath, he'd written:

"What we carry becomes who we are."

"Damn," I said. "That's clean."

He nodded. "It's true."

I just stood there a second, looking at him.

At the work.

At the *man he was becoming.*

Later, I sat at my desk with the sun coming in low through the windows. A long, gold light that made everything look softer.

I opened a folder I hadn't touched in months—old papers, early budgets, drafts of grant applications. Near the back, tucked between a half-finished curriculum plan and a Post-it from Simone that read *"stop overthinking it, Dad,"* was the note Darius gave me back in college.

He had written it on the back of a flyer for some student showcase I can't even remember.

He handed it to me the day I embarrassed both of us by snapping on a vendor who'd botched the food delivery. I thought I was standing up for the team.

But Darius had just watched me quietly, waited for the day to pass, then passed me this:

"You don't have to run everything to matter. Some people show up just by being solid. Be that."

It haunted me for years.

Because I didn't get it then.

I thought showing up meant being loud, being first, being the fix.

Now?

Now I knew better.

Solid doesn't mean still.
Solid means steady.

I leaned back in the chair, paper still in hand, and let out a breath I didn't know I'd been holding.

That's what this whole thing had become.

Not a project.
Not a job.

But a kind of **promise** I was making to myself—
and keeping.

By late afternoon, the space began to shift.

Rodney packed up. A few younger kids floated in to
clean brushes and work on their mural section. I
gave pointers when asked, but mostly I watched.

Let them do their thing.

The way Darius used to watch me and think I didn't
notice.

Alexis showed up just before five.

She stepped inside like she lived there, which—if
I'm being real—she kind of did now. Not her mail.
Not her name on the lease.

But her **presence** lived here.

She crossed her arms and leaned in the doorway.

"You always this predictable?"

I turned, smirking. "Only on weekdays ending in Y."

We met halfway across the room. I kissed her forehead, handed her a bottle of water.

"You been here all day?" she asked.

"Mostly."

"Thinking about what's next?"

"A little."

"What'd you come up with?"

I shrugged. "I'm starting to think the map don't come with a legend. You just mark where you've been, and hope the line makes sense later."

She smiled.

"That's not bad."

"I learned it from this woman I've been seeing."

"She sounds wise."

"She's something."

We walked around the mural space—she traced her fingers across the edges of a piece one of the middle schoolers had painted: a skyline made of books.

"Kids are wild," she said. "This kind of imagination?"

"They just needed somewhere to put it."

We reached the far wall. A new panel. Blank.

"You saving this?" she asked.

"Yeah."

"For what?"

"I don't know yet."

She nodded.

"Maybe you don't need to."

We stood there in silence.

Not waiting.

Just standing.

Like we'd finally found a way to be still together, without needing to narrate it.

That's the thing I came to understand.

The map isn't fixed.

It doesn't show up in one piece.

You draw it as you go.

Each choice. Each beat. Each failure. Each forgiveness.
Each face that loved you. Each one that didn't.

Every time you doubled back.
Every time you finally let someone in.
Every time you stopped trying to be more and just became *enough*.

The map was never a direction.

It was a **record**.

And I wasn't lost anymore.

Epilogue

"We been aligned and assigned to change /
Rearrange your molecules like Dr. Strange."
— Q-Tip, "Renaissance Rap"

It was one of those warm, early spring evenings that didn't need music to feel like a soundtrack.

Inside The Spot, the walls buzzed—not from speakers, but from people. Energy. Voices. Kids showing off their work, some parents standing back in awe, others asking where to sign up their younger ones. A few teachers from the local middle school were in the back, chatting up Rodney about expanding his mural into the rec center's lobby.

Rodney looked taller these days.

Not physically.
Spiritually.

Like he was no longer pulling from Darius's light—he was making his own.

I stood near the front door with a bottle of water and a full heart.

Everywhere I looked, there was a piece of something we built.

The panel that used to be blank was now filled in—three sets of hands. One adult, two smaller. Palms open, light flowing through the spaces between the fingers. Beneath it, in clean white script: **"Legacy doesn't end—it expands."**

Rodney had painted it.
He didn't say much when he finished it.
Just nodded at me once like, *yeah, I see it too.*

Simone arrived midway through the evening, her usual quiet grace making way before her.

She wore a light denim jacket, curls out, big hoops. She gave me a hug that lasted just long enough to whisper:

"This is beautiful, Dad. You've really done something here."

"I'm trying."

"You're doing."

She stepped back, then added with that sly sparkle she got from her mother:

"And I might have someone I want to bring next time."

I raised an eyebrow. "Yeah?"

She smiled. "We'll see."

Alexis found me later near the back wall, where we'd stacked chairs earlier in the day.

She didn't say much—just leaned against me with that weightless kind of love. The kind that doesn't ask for anything but room to stay.

I kissed the side of her temple, and she looked up at me.

"You alright?" she asked.

"Yeah," I said. "I am."

We sat down together on the edge of the small stage and just watched.

The laughter.
The shared stories.
The legacy in motion.

There was a moment when I felt it—not like a jolt, but like a click.

Like I had finally found rhythm with **my life**.

Not surviving it.
Not hiding in it.
Just *moving through it* with both feet on the ground.

I thought about Q-Tip's line—

*"We been aligned and assigned to change /
Rearrange your molecules like Dr. Strange."*

That's what this felt like.
Like every part of me had been shaken up, realigned, and then **stitched back together with intention**.

Not the same Malik.

Not better or worse.

Just... **awake**.

The night wound down. Chairs scraped gently across the floor. Leftover cookies disappeared one napkin at a time. Kids huddled around phones playing beats, arguing about who had next.

I walked Alexis out, her hand tucked into mine.

As we stood outside under the dim glow of the parking lot light, she looked over and said, "You proud?"

"I am," I said. "Of all of it."

Then I added, quieter:

"You're everything I dream about, talk about / Walk around and brag about."

She grinned. "C.L. Smooth?"

I nodded.

"Sounded better than you saying you're in love."

"I figured you already knew that part."

"I did," she said, then leaned in. "But I like the remix."

And with that, she drove off into the slow, safe dark.
And I stood there for a moment longer, hands in my pockets, heart wide open.

The map?

It's not finished.
Not even close.

But the legend's clear now.
And every step forward—every *searching*, every
fight, every *loop back to center*—

It's all part of the way forward.

Musical References & Acknowledgments

This work is a tribute to Hip-Hop as an art form, a cultural force, and a personal compass. The chapter titles and select lyrical excerpts throughout this novel are drawn from seminal Hip-Hop tracks that shaped the voice, perspective, and emotional arc of this story.

These references are included with deep admiration and respect for the original creators and their impact. Every effort has been made to honor their legacy through thoughtful, transformative use.

All rights to song lyrics, titles, and musical content remain the sole property of their respective artists, writers, publishers, and rights holders.

Referenced Artists (alphabetically):

- A Tribe Called Quest
- Big Pun
- Black Star
- C.L. Smooth
- Common
- Doug E. Fresh & The Get Fresh Crew
- EPMD
- Gang Starr
- Mos Def

- Nas
- OutKast
- Pete Rock & C.L. Smooth
- Q-Tip
- Slick Rick
- Souls of Mischief
- Talib Kweli & Hi-Tek
- The Pharcyde
- Pharoahe Monch
- The Roots ft. Erykah Badu
- Wu-Tang Clan

Fair Use Statement:

This novel contains brief excerpts of copyrighted song lyrics for the purposes of literary homage, cultural commentary, and character development. These references are used under fair use principles and are not intended for commercial exploitation or to infringe on the rights of the original creators. No ownership is claimed.

With Gratitude:

To the artists, producers, and poets who told the truth in rhythm. Thank you for soundtracking our lives—and giving us language for our becoming.

About the Author

Perry D. Jones is a storyteller rooted in rhythm, memory, and meaning. With a voice shaped by family, faith, and the golden age of hip hop, he writes stories that explore Black masculinity, vulnerability, and the long road to healing.

The Map is his debut literary novel — a deeply personal coming-of-age story about a man navigating love, grief, fatherhood, and the power of music to hold us together. Through the eyes of Malik Patterson, Perry invites readers to walk the path of transformation — one chapter, one track at a time.

In addition to *The Map* and its companion novel *The Legend*, Perry is the author of the historical fiction novels *Archer: A Discovered Legacy* and *Dicey: A Legacy of Strength*, which trace the resilience and resistance of one Black family across generations.

When he's not writing, Perry is tracing family lines through genealogy, researching African American history, and building Synergy Books — a home for stories with soul.

"Act like you know — not now, but right now." — A Tribe Called Quest

Also by Perry D. Jones

• *The Legend* — The companion novel to *The Map*, continuing Malik Patterson's journey of love, family, and self-discovery, set to a soulful new soundtrack.

• *Archer: A Discovered Legacy* — A historical fiction novel tracing a family's pursuit of identity, education, and survival across generations.

• *Dicey: A Legacy of Strength* — The companion to *Archer*, revealing the powerful story of a woman whose legacy is rooted in defiance, love, and legacy.

Learn more at http://www.synergybooks.co/

Reading Group Questions for *The Map*

1. *The Map* uses Hip-Hop not just as a backdrop, but as a storytelling tool. What role does music play in Malik's emotional evolution? Did any particular song or reference stand out to you personally?

2. Malik is at a turning point at 49. What does "coming of age" look like for someone later in life? How does that reframe the way we think about personal growth?

3. What's the significance of Malik's relationship with his daughter Simone? How do their moments together reflect larger themes of generational understanding and healing?

4. Darius's absence is a constant presence. How does grief show up in Malik's day-to-day choices and relationships?

5. How does the dynamic between Malik and Gerald evolve, and what does that say about father-son legacies?

6. How does Malik use "The Spot" (his community center) as a vessel for his own healing? What does the center represent?

7. What do you think the book says about vulnerability in Black men? Did Malik's internal reflections resonate with your experience or challenge your perspective?

8. Which scene or chapter stuck with you the most emotionally — and why?

9. How did the chapter titles (named after hip-hop songs) shape the mood of each section?

10. Do you see Malik as someone who found what he was looking for? Or is he still searching?
11. If you could sit with Malik and ask him one question, what would it be?
12. After finishing *The Map*, what did "the map" ultimately represent to you?

Appendix

Hip Hop Tracklist & Chapter Index

Chapter	Song Title	Artist
Prologue	The Show	Doug E. Fresh & The Get Fresh Crew
1	Can I Kick It?	A Tribe Called Quest
2	T.R.O.Y.	Pete Rock & CL Smooth
3	Ex-Girl to Next Girl	Gang Starr
4	Electric Relaxation	A Tribe Called Quest
5	Children's Story	Slick Rick
6	Respiration	Black Star
7	The Light	Common
8	C.R.E.A.M.	Wu-Tang Clan
9	Umi Says	Mos Def
10	Memory Lane	Nas
11	Still Not a Player	Big Pun
12	Ms. Jackson	OutKast
13	Runnin'	The Pharcyde
14	Moment of Truth	Gang Starr

Chapter	Song Title	Artist
15	I Used to Love H.E.R.	Common
16	God Lives Through	A Tribe Called Quest
17	The Blast	Talib Kweli & Hi-Tek
18	You Got Me	The Roots ft. Erykah Badu
19	Love Is	Common
20	93 'Til Infinity	Souls of Mischief
21	Rewind	Nas
22	I Wonder	Kanye West
23	1nce Again	A Tribe Called Quest
24	We Fight/We Love	Q-Tip
25	The Map	(Original Chapter Title)
Epilogue	(Renaissance Rap/Searching)	Q-Tip/Pete Rock & CL Smooth